CORE RULESET

CORE RULESET

By

Timothy Bryan

"Man is mortal, and as the professor so rightly said, mortality can come so suddenly"

-The New Ivan, Mikhail Bulgakov's
The Master and Margarita

Table of Contents

Chapter One

Against the night's opaque and overcast background, where light from the moon shone sporadically through coursing pockets of luminous clouds, a cavernous office building stood on the skyline of a huge office park. Situated next to two smaller buildings, the main structure was a striking edifice of corporatism, offering a wide view from its plentiful windows of the surrounding countryside and the expansive, dotted-light suburbs of California's Central Valley.

The inside of the building was largely empty and dark, but even at this late time of night, in a period when most people had already eaten dinner and retired for the night, a few conscientious souls still attended to their workstations. These hardy workers clacked away at their keyboards, staring at luminescent screens in the darkness as they tried to catch up on the endless duties reserved for those whose time was less valuable than their mission of efficiency.

On the top floor of the structure was the executive suite of offices. Here, illumination was stronger, with lights belting out sufficient lumens to make the refined portion of the building seem like the stellar core of a minor star. In this well-lit area were expensive wood and designer furniture, matching the pricey motif of shiny nameplates that adorned well-oiled doors running the length of the penthouse location.

One door in particular was at the best location of the elite environment, recessed to allow an area in front of it to have a personal secretary and its own custom self-serve coffee bar. Its plaque read *CEO Benelux Capital R. Darby*, and just then, it was pushed open as its occupant exited the room.

Reginald Darby strode from his office, looking intently about as his vision adjusted to the powerful light. In his late forties, the bespectacled CEO was a man whose white skin tone made him appear almost like an albino, but his pale complexion was also offset by fierce eyes and a domineering countenance. Attentive and intense, he exuded the "A" in a typical type-A personality. Quick-witted and supremely intelligent, his invasive stare had a way of lingering on a person until all their secrets were revealed, either by open admission of what he wanted to know or by simply exposing their secrets due to a weaker capacity for hiding thoughts or intentions.

Dressed in a dark sweatsuit, Darby walked to his secretary's desk, where he looked down at his personal assistant with inquiring eyes. Mary, an officious middle-aged woman of considerable girth and extreme organizational prowess, briefly met his gaze from behind her set of 32-inch computer monitors.

"Mary, do you suppose you could find the financials for the Newton acquisition?" asked Darby, sounding a bit miffed. "I can't seem to locate their proposed financing for the restructure."

Nodding, Mary responded with a subservient smile. "I'll dig them up and forward them to you. Are you going home, or will you be coming back? Should I order some food for delivery?"

Thinking for a moment, Darby shook his head. "I'll finish my run, then be on my way home. I hope the traffic is better tonight; those bloodsuckers from Caltrans are milking every bit of that highway project. Must be nice to be paid so you can continually extend your job—instead of seeing it through to completion."

Mary merely nodded, returning to her screen and opening a calendar application to plan for the next day's schedule. She made it a point to not engage Darby when he expounded on such matters, whether he was right or wrong. In fact, the older Mary got, the more she realized that such notions of correctness or being wrong were often entirely beside the point; what mattered most was for such people to feel important, feared, and admired.

Looking down at his fitness watch, Darby pressed the dial to monitor his heart rate, which currently beat at "65" in a digital format. Approving of the number, he moved to the reception area to stretch his legs in preparation for a jog.

Loosening up, Darby's eyes caught on a television that ran uninterrupted throughout the day and was mounted in the corner of the room. Irritated, he spoke in an impatient tone. "Mary, could you turn that drivel up for a moment?"

In the background of the TV image was a factory of low-wage workers assembling electrical boards and preparing them for shipment in cardboard boxes. When Mary tapped the remote, the sound from an unseen male business newscaster flooded the quiet office space. "Benelux Capital has not responded to requests for comment. Despite several thousand jobs being at risk, the company has not addressed growing concerns that their recent acquisition will force cost-cutting…"

After making a cutting motion across his neck, Mary quickly muted the volume in response to Darby's request to end the intrusive sound. There was silence for a time as Darby finished his preparations for exercise while Mary returned to her work.

Finishing his stretch, Darby leaned closer to Mary, not so much in a desire for actual interaction, but instead to never miss the opportunity to lecture those around him. "I tire of all these hit jobs. Those reporters are full of shit because they certainly did contact me—they just didn't like what I had to say. Apparently, they would prefer a company go bankrupt instead of adapting to the market. They would also prefer five thousand unemployed workers over the five hundred I'm proposing."

Mary smiled deferentially at the mini speech, offering a dutiful poker face to his explanation. She had spent a lifetime dealing with powerful people, and whatever the content of their opinions, she knew the best way to get along was by letting them listen to their own viewpoints, either by acting like a like-minded person or just nodding in feigned agreement as they pontificated. Besides, unemployment for those workers was a horrible thing, but as her checks from this well-paying job cleared her account without error, she was inclined to think her own life without a job would be far worse.

Contented for the moment, Darby stepped back and faced the elevator. Pressing the button, he took a deep breath and tried his best nice-guy voice. "Okay then, don't forward anything else to me—unless it's important. And…have a good night."

When the elevator door opened, he stepped into the relaxing music of the executive-level-only car, not bothering to wait for a reply to his well wishes.

#

The lobby was well-lit but mostly empty at this time of night, with only two bored security guards passing their time in the window-enclosed main reception area. Seeing Darby, the building's most important tenant at this late time of night, each stood from playing with their phones and tried to appear professional by acting diligent and aware. It wasn't like they had anything else to do as they whittled away their monotonous shift, but appearances were always important.

Frowning at the spectacle, Darby was at least happy to see that they were not asleep at their duties. Waving absently to the burly uniformed personnel, he padded across the shiny floor, his running shoes squeaking as he made his way out the main door. As the immaculately clean door closed gently behind him, Darby was quickly lost from the cover of lights that showcased the entrance to the enormous lobby.

Outside, the corporate center was an affluent area. Numerous lampposts circled the exterior of the property, and a cushioned running path twisted under the series of lights as it worked its way around the extensive perimeter portion of the well-maintained grounds. All manner of trees and fields of grass surrounded his way forward, offering pleasant running conditions, even in the near darkness. As if on cue, the chatter of crickets added their pitch of nighttime noise to the otherwise-quiet night, making the environment seem more rural with their repetitive chorus.

Glancing at his watch, Darby slipped expensive Bluetooth earbuds into his ears and breathed deeply, taking in the dry and still-warm air from the summer day's endless blast of sweltering heat. One thing about the Sacramento area was that it often made the Middle East's weather patterns seem positively normal in comparison, so it was always best to exercise during the lower temperatures of darkness.

Holding up his phone to access a favorite playlist on his most-liked music app, Darby started some classical music, the type that often inspired creative types as they went about their creative work. In Darby's case, the creativity consisted of trying to beat his best running time around the entirety of the property, and his excellent cardiovascular health meant such a goal was often achieved. He seemed to make a best new time on several occasions every month.

Darby removed his glasses and tucked them into the pocket of his svelte workout clothes. Smiling, he started his jog, moving at a brisk pace into the uneven darkness ahead. By only one hundred yards into his rapid clip, his controlled breaths were practiced and professional, and his continued exercise would assure yet another healthy end to his self-important workday.

Life is good, Darby thought, and as he set a torrid pace around his domain, he wondered how the little people ever got used to the tedium of their worker-bee lives.

#

The music continued its steady and violinic whine in Darby's ears, coming to a crescendo and making him pump his legs faster due to his inspiration at the instruments' wonderful pitch. Fifteen minutes into his run, Darby had a pleasant sheen of sweat percolating on his face, and his body felt alive as he pushed himself on the now-remote trail. Focusing ahead, Darby increased his pace to a point he felt would surely have won him a medal—somewhere or other. Glancing at his watch, he noted his heart rate had now climbed to "160."

As he labored along, Darby briefly wondered why he had never pursued a professional sport. As a teen, he had briefly toyed with soccer, and as he considered that, he realized he could have been a professional with it if he had so chosen.

Darby's work ethic and intelligence made everything he did a successful venture, and he had frankly never put his mind to something and then failed. He knew that seemed arrogant to others, but what was the point of lying? Some people were born to be garbage truck drivers, and they could even form a successful life out of doing that job, so Darby felt little need to apologize about what he was good at…which tended to be everything.

Coming back to the moment, he quickly understood why he had to drop his foray into soccer infamy: he simply didn't have the time. Acing his SATs into college, he had then received a full-ride all the way through his MBA at Harvard. Exiting his studies after more perfect academic results, he had formed a hedge fund with some classmates and began to ascend the ranks of the ultra-successful and ultra-rich.

By the time he was thirty, Darby had made his first hundred million, and when his forties arrived, he had expanded his personal moniker of financial wizard to include the title of billionaire. Few men he knew sought out or achieved more in a shorter time than he, and Darby knew every inch of his success was earned and legitimate, which was a point that he often made to the few "friends" he interacted with. While others relied on nepotism for success, Darby did it by and for himself.

Still, Darby had felt a little dejected about success as of late. His fortune, while impressive, had never cleared the eleven-figure range, and that was a goal he had set out to specifically attain by the time he would turn fifty the following January.

Truth was, unless an early investment went very well when a medical company went public in two months, he would have to accept that goal would need to be moved back. As he rounded a bend in the jogging path, he frowned at that hideous thought of something he was entirely uncomfortable with: prospective failure—missing a firm goal he had set for himself.

Darby suddenly slowed his pace to a curious walk. Up ahead, around some trees that stood aside his personal trail, was a large splotch of darkness. Glancing to the light posts in that area, he saw they offered no illumination from their custom and very expensive frames. Because they there powered by solar energy, and this area always got plenty of sunlight, Darby knew something was amiss. He had paid to ensure his night jogging journeys were always accompanied by sufficient brightness, so to encounter this outage was unusual. *Strange.*

Walking closer to the dim area, Darby's gaze moved to focus on the bulbs of the nearest two lamps. Staring up, he crossed his arms in frustration, trying to figure out whose ass he was going to chew out for this maintenance shortfall.

Unfortunately, Darby had recently fired the old guy who oversaw such things in the past, as the doddering geezer had been unable to keep up with Darby's strict demands. Sighing, Darby realized he would just have to find a new person—and pay him more, too, if need be. He was not a cheap man, and the thing he liked most about money was the more you paid, the better help you tended to acquire.

From behind, the crunch of gravel under a heavy step got Darby's attention. Startled, he spun around to see a man standing near one of the custom benches placed periodically along the trail. Next to the bench was one of the shining lampposts, and it cast bright light down upon the figure of this sudden and strange nighttime observer.

The man was covered from head to toe in a huge cloak made up of some animal skin or similar material. A hood covered his face, and he stared at Darby from beneath the dark material's creepy confines.

Even worse on the weirdness scale, the man was enormous, easily the largest individual Darby had ever seen in person. Almost in a *gigantism* sort of way, his huge frame was off-kilter, like his body was proportioned strangely, with varying parts of his physique too large for the whole.

Taking out his eyeglasses, Darby slipped them on in an attempt to get a closer look at the man. Oddly, the man's jaw seemed to protrude in such a way as to make his face underneath the hood misshapen—grotesque even. Only an odd beard of black-matted hair protruded from the portion of his dark-skinned jaw that was visible, but what could be seen appeared revolting.

Never one to shrink from anything, Darby spoke up, trying to keep his tone rational and commanding. "Can I help you?"

The stranger didn't answer and instead tilted his immense head, as if he was measuring up Darby for some purpose.

"Do you work in the complex?" asked Darby, already knowing the answer to be *no*. "I haven't seen you here before."

The large man still stayed quiet, merely shaking his head in response. Darby got the impression that he was being evaluated by a predator, almost like this man was a big-game hunter looking for the perfect specimen to hang on a well-appointed wall within a hunting lodge.

Oddly, in a flash of hysterical imagination that jumped into mind, Darby pictured his own shocked face and head mounted on some serial killer's wall. He wasn't prone to such flights of crazy mental behavior, but Darby nevertheless became more worried with each passing moment, as if something like that peculiar inner hallucination could indeed occur.

Feeling increasingly uneasy, Darby decided that discretion was the better part of valor. Walking away from the bizarre individual, he was soon within the cone of darkness down the trail, where the lights were mysteriously out. When he glanced back to ensure he wasn't followed, he was shocked to see the man was no longer there; the area below and around the light post and bench was now completely empty.

Darby had enough of this strangeness, and he moved his eyes to the front expectantly. Breaking into a full sprint, he rushed through the darkness towards the next series of functioning lampposts seventy yards in the distance. His frantic pace now ensured a new personal record for his jogging exploits, but at the moment, that treasured milestone didn't seem very important.

#

Emerging from the last line of trees, Darby stumbled into the open, where he was surrounded by a well-tended and extensive lawn. After coming to a stop, he breathed in rasps for several long moments as he collected his raging thoughts into something like a normal frame of mind. In time, his breathing subsided, and he looked ahead with relief at the familiar surroundings.

In front of him were two of the smaller structures in the series of office buildings that made up the core of his business empire. Each was a few stories high, and they housed everything from the maintenance functions for the property to classrooms by which many of his associate firms trained their personnel across several industries. Surrounded by lights, the property was brightly illuminated and controlled by a state-of-the-art security system, one that was supposed to be the best in class.

Inhaling deeply, Darby produced a mobile phone and speed-dialed security. He was one of those people that prepared for everything, and he kept every phone number of consequence within easy reach for any contingency that presented itself.

The main building's officer-in-charge answered immediately.

Darby spoke into the receiver with the tone of one who was there to give information, not wait for excuses. "Security? This is Reginald Darby…yes that one, from the top floor. Listen, I don't wish to tell you how to do your job, but there's some lunatic near the south jogging path—in an area where there is supposed to be exactly nobody. He is…a very large man and wearing some kind of gray furry long coat."

Walking closer to the first of the two smaller buildings, Darby stared at a gazebo that was attached to the side of it. It was a place to take breaks or have cookouts for team-building exercises. Listening to his phone, he shook his head impatiently. "No, I've never seen him before, which is kind of why I thought you should know about it. I would have thought your cameras would have allowed this knowledge to reach you without my call, but now…here we are."

Speaking over an apparently defensive and garbled response, Darby raised his voice. "Please make sure you find him and see that he is escorted from the property. Most importantly, be careful, because he didn't appear friendly. Don't hesitate to call the police if he offers you any trouble."

Cutting off the man, Darby hung up the phone. As he put it away, he smiled to himself at the interplay with the guard. It wasn't often that he got to play the part of a crime fighter, and it felt pretty good to sic the lazy bastards on some mutant homeless guy who had somehow found his way onto the company's property. He kind of felt like a conquering general and, in fact, mentally added that job title to the professions he would have excelled at if he had the time in the past to pursue such a career.

Chuckling, Darby realized being the next Dwight D. Eisenhower may not have been as fun as if he had become the world's premier soccer player, but it probably would have suited his talents better. He despised the military in general, but he did like the idea he could have had people locked up if they disobeyed him. All forms of personal power appealed to him, but the kind that allowed insubordination to be punished by jail time was positively bursting with possibilities.

Smiling to himself, Darby began his jog again, making certain to angle towards the nearest building and stay within the plentiful light that ran along its exterior. When he got near the first of the structures, the huge man, the one that had so ruffled him earlier, stepped from behind a small storage building.

This dark and enormous man now held a huge battle axe, one that was nearly as long as Darby himself. Stepping toward Darby, the gigantic individual moved quickly, far faster than Darby would have imagined or hoped for. As he rushed forward, Darby stumbled to the side, trying to veer away from the oncoming danger.

Darby screamed in awestruck fear, sounding like a terrified child being chased in a freakish nightmare. "Whaahht? Fuck, help me, somebody help."

Kicking out with a monstrous foot, the attacker sent Darby reeling, and the desperate CEO spun and flopped in the middle of a raised grassy area. Scurrying to the right, Darby was quick to recover, and he flung himself under a barbecue that was cemented in place at the edge of the communal area.

Raising his weapon, the attacker's wicked axe swung down at Darby, who just made it to safety by getting behind the small-but-firm barbecue. The axe slammed into the cooker, cutting through half of its metal parts and getting stuck. The colossal man yanked on the fierce weapon, trying to pull it free.

Struggling to gain his balance, Darby tried to distance himself from the brute. Falling down, he rolled upright and stumbled, then began to accelerate. Surging ahead, his feet found traction, and he made a dash toward the tree line in a desperate bid for safety.

With a revolting THUD, the airborne axe buried itself in Darby's back. Thrown from thirty feet, the vicious blade had been cast sideways, where it found its mark from the maniacal aggressor. Crumbling to the grass, Darby was incapacitated by the blow, his spine severed under the brutal assault of the masterfully thrown weapon.

Grunting nonsensically, Darby tried to pull himself along the ground. With legs that didn't function, he looked like a bug that had half its limbs smashed and had become useless. His groans of pain were sad and confused, and in his mind, Darby imagined it was someone else that was going through this trauma—almost like he was watching a cartoonish display of some other soul's wretched demise.

Walking quickly to Darby, the behemoth yanked the axe from his back with a sickly thrashing sound. Not able to pull himself away, Darby flipped over and stared up at the attacker, looking at the uncovered and unseen face of his assailant with terrified eyes.

Seeing something he couldn't understand, Darby's sobs of pain moved to shrieks of helpless and unrestrained fear. Incomprehension colored his features, and for the first time in his life, he was faced with a situation he couldn't comprehend or react to. Holding up a quivering arm, he tried to ward off what was coming for him.

Swinging the axe down, the stranger severed the arm and cleaved the long and sharp edge into Darby's upper torso. Mortally wounded, Darby arched his back and coughed blood in spurts, trying to get oxygen into lungs that no longer worked. His eyes moved around the area, spasmodically looking at the manicured grass and buildings that he had built and overseen. He alone had created this all, and now it had come to this, killed at his own company by this…thing.

As darkness closed in on his worldly perception, a weird final thought emerged from Darby's mind, one that was borne from a life spent pursuing self-gratification and power: *who will spend all my money?*

Wrenching the weapon free, blood spilled from the immense and jagged wound, but Darby had already departed from living considerations. His lifeless eyes focused to the side, as if he had found something interesting in the grass to gaze at.

His work completed, the merciless attacker hefted his weapon on his immense shoulder and began to walk toward the trees where Darby had recently emerged. Apparently unconcerned about his crime, the assailant was in no hurry as he ambled away from the bloody scene. While he paced away in a jaunting, relaxed fashion, sandaled and hairy feet were visible below the killer's flowing and oversized cloak.

Next to the body, an electronic pinging erupted from the fitness watch Darby so assiduously used to ensure his peak physical condition in life. Still attached to his severed and twitching arm, the digital screen blinked a heart rate of "0" in concert with the beeping sound.

Chapter Two

The dusty interior of the garage looked like a cluttered flea market. Tools were suspended on hooks across several walls, and buckets of screws, nails and assorted plastic toys were piled on poorly constructed shelves underneath the rusting handsaws and hedge clippers.

In the rafters across the ceiling were crammed a multitude of fishing rods and camping supplies, along with burlap bags full of little league baseball equipment. Cobwebs were spread amongst other possessions that ranged from old pet carriers to boxes of musty clothing, and throughout the rest of the floor space was an old treadmill, several stacks of roofing tiles, and piles of business magazines that were last relevant during the Clinton administration.

Though of substantial size, there didn't appear to be space for an actual car inside the garage, even a small one. If a long-abandoned Walmart had sneezed its dilapidated contents into a substantial room like this, the various items muddling the area would have been the result.

Sitting in the corner of the room, looking down over a press of some kind, was Dani Isaksson. Forty-five years old, with close-cropped dark hair and an attractive face that seemed to always be amused, she focused intently on her work.

Moving a lever down, she watched carefully as an empty pistol cartridge was mated in her press with a bullet. The resultant live ammunition, crimped into a deadly new projectile in standard .40 caliber size, made her smile, and she approvingly held it up to light streaming through a nearby dirty window.

Setting the bullet down, Dani carefully placed it next in a row of other ammunition already created, and she exhaled with contentment at the culmination of her reloading experience. Standing, she stretched her back and looked about the garage, reminding herself for the thousandth time this summer that this place really needed to be cleaned up and organized.

Dani cursed herself for her lack of tidiness, wondering what gene allowed a person to actually care enough to keep old things in order. Frowning, she realized that whatever or wherever it was, she decidedly didn't possess it.

A tap tap tap on the garage door brought her out of her thoughts, and she scowled at the dirty and never-used front entrance to her garage hideaway. "Hideo, that better not be you."

Silence came in answer to her voice, followed by a man clearing his throat. "How did you know it was me?"

Shrugging and running a frustrated hand through her short hair, Dani raised her voice in irritation. "Who else knocks on a random garage door? Especially when I leave for vacation tomorrow?"

There was a hesitation before a reply. "Yeah…about that…"

Alarmed, Dani slapped a button on the wall, and the garage door began to creak open. As the seemingly ancient portal rose with a horrendous squeaking sound, light flooded inside, making Dani squint as she faced her visitor.

Standing on her cracked driveway was Hideo Smith. In his mid-thirties and dressed in a cheap suit, his Asian-American features were somewhat revolted as he stared into the chaotic interior. He stepped tentatively inside, as if he might catch the plague from the disordered environment.

"This is a dump," said Hideo, scrunching up his nose. "How do you know where anything is?"

"It's a rigorous filing system. Takes years to learn," Dani deadpanned. "What the hell are you doing here?"

Moving his gaze over her reloading efforts, Hideo walked close to Dani. He offered her a mischievous smile as he held up a thick folder. Dropping it on her workbench, he made a point of speaking slowly. "We…got a homicide over at the Tech Center. Some muckety-muck got axed. Literally."

Frowning, Dani picked up the folder. She squinted as she rummaged through several photos of the recently deceased Reginald Darby, raising her eyebrows in surprise at the condition of the corpse and manner of death. Flipping through the pages, she read most of the attached report and took in the pertinent details of the slaying.

Finally closing the folder, she faced her bored-looking partner. "And this affects me because…?"

Hideo grinned in reply, one of those grins that made a person want to choke him—especially the person he now faced. "Captain Alvarez says he needs it solved, ahora…which is 'now' to you and me. Despite his better judgment, he asked for us to make it happen. Don't know what he was thinking, but here I am."

Hideo punctuated the last statement with a celebratory expression, like he was P.T. Barnum announcing the beginning of a new show that was predestined to succeed.

Dani's features deflated. Looking around the garage, she motioned to some of the camping and fishing gear. It wasn't clear which gear was ready for travel and which gear had been packed away for decades. "What about my trip to Alaska?"

Hideo's smile grew more pronounced. "The needs of the public come first, soldier."

"You're a prick, Hideo."

"I've heard that before—too often, in fact," said Hideo, and he motioned to her reloading bench as he changed the subject nonchalantly. "If you were planning to fish, what's with making bullets?"

"The bears up there like to fish, too. There are thousands of 'em prowling the forests…creeks…rivers. You can never be too careful."

Hideo nodded, then smiled insincerely. "Then it's good I got here in time. Preventing your trip may have just saved your life. You should be thanking me—and the department."

Sighing, Dani chuckled. After dropping the folder on a bench, she glanced outside, looking at the burgeoning sunlight that was heating up the asphalt street around her humble house in her quiet working-class neighborhood.

Shaking her head, Dani wondered how long this case was going to take. She also considered her soon-to-be-canceled trip and tried to remember why she even contemplated going to Alaska in the first place. She couldn't fish for shit and hated bears.

#

Metal figures stood around the imaginary battle scene. Werewolves, wizards, and an assortment of action-figure monsters vied for room in the large and clear-sided display case. Most were painted in bright colors and evinced a world where spells and swordplay determined the winner, at least in the imaginations of their prospective owners.

A chubby hand reached into the case, plucking a grayish and unpainted figure from the gaggle of mismatched combatants. This particular character had a long, flowing cloak, an ugly half-dog face, and feet covered by leather-looking sandals. Also, a long and deadly battle axe was cradled over the monster's beefy shoulder.

Terry Brandt, thirty-nine and the embodiment of geekdom, held the character up, his eyes fixated on the figure. Terry had the paunchiness and bearing of one who made triple cheeseburgers a regular part of his training regimen, and along with increasing his non-existent trips to the gym, he should probably have worked on adapting a healthier lifestyle.

Keeping his fighter in hand, he paced to the counter of the comic bookstore and held up his upcoming purchase with almost religious respect. Gesturing at the figure, he set it in front of the store's owner.

Michael Badger was in his forties, dishevelled, and seemed to enjoy his status as a lifelong connoisseur of all games aligned with the teenaged and younger crowd. His eyes held youthful appreciation and joy for what he did, even if the wrinkles and circles under them indicated an upcoming appointment with middle age. He showed his approval of Terry's new acquisition with a thoughtful nod.

"An excellent choice," Badger said, showing teeth that could have used whitening a decade or more ago. "That particular half-orc is a fine addition to any party. He can really deal out the damage. MONDO damage."

Terry grunted in agreement. "I'll take 'em. I'll work on him before the game tomorrow night. If I put in the time, I should have 'em ready when it starts."

Chewing on his lip, Badger glanced around his shop, where a handful of young and not-so-young men poked through comic books, castles, and games, each entranced with their own version of nerd bliss in a sea of imaginary entertainment.

Seeing nobody was listening in, Badger lowered his voice into a conspiratorial whisper. "Thought I would let you know. A new series of Elves is coming out, and I thought it might be time for you to refresh your lineup? They'll be here next week."

Terry's already dreamy gaze heightened into rapt attention, and his eyes flashed the unmistakable eagerness of a true believer. "Hell yeah. Think they'll have a mage in it? Always hard to get magic-users in the Elven race."

Badger nodded sagely. "True. Nobody likes to play 'em. Guys always want to play an Elven Ranger…or be an ambidextrous fighter. Don't know exactly what's comin', but you get the first crack at the shipment—just like always."

It was now Terry's turn to avoid giving away a secret. He glanced around and lowered his tone. "The good thing about collecting stuff is, when nobody else wants it, you can always get the good stuff."

"What do you mean?"

"Well," replied Terry. "Think of lobsters."

"The ocean, crabby things?" asked Badger, looking perplexed.

"Yeah, exactly," Terry said, focusing on Badger to make his point. "Way back when, they used to feed 'em to prisoners. You went to the slammer, and they fed you lobster—they were like rats of the sea. Then, one day, BOOM, they're a delicacy. Now, all the rich folks spend tons of money to serve them for every special occasion."

Confused, Badger tilted his head. "But, if you would have collected lobsters for all that time, when they became popular, you would've just had a bunch of broken shells, right?"

Rolling his eyes, Terry showed an empathetic grin to the gaming guru. "No, you would've had years of tasty lobster that cost nothing. Don't you see? It's all about supply and demand."

Looking surprised and not quite informed, Badger nevertheless nodded, acquiescing to the fuzzy logic. "Not sure how you could eat Elven mage figures, but I think I get your point."

Keeping his smile, Terry merely gloated as he considered his good fortune for the day. Looking down at his new half-orc play figure, his face beamed like a proud father.

Chapter Three

The office building and the surrounding tech center looked much more inviting in the light of day. The well-constructed white building gleamed with the afternoon's decreasing sunlight, and its front reflected light from rows of clean windows. Whatever the intent or results of Benelux Capital as a business entity, the place offered a snappy and pleasant place of work.

In an extensive parking lot in front of the three buildings, a mix of various vehicles, from expensive BMWs to functional Ford Fiestas, showed the varied pay rates of employees that made their work at the company. In the front row, there were also several electric vehicles that made use of the company's preference for "going green" to access free charging for those willing to splash outrageous sums for cars needing their power from the electrical grid.

Pulling their unmarked police car into a spot marked "Reserved," Hideo grimaced at the expensive complex and its pristine condition, while at his side Dani took in the attractive work environment with an opposite and approving nod.

Stepping free from the vehicle, Dani's gaze swept the larger building, and she admired its wide view as she contemplated the wealth and organization that had brought the business and its employees into existence.

Dani was always interested in the formation of corporations, and it amazed her how a business could evolve from essentially nothing into a world-conquering company. She remembered a time when the name "Google" meant exactly nothing, and even vaguely recalled a period when IBM's personal computers were synonymous with the actual underlying technology that constituted "PCs." Now, Google ran half the world by search, ads, or phones, while IBM was…well, she didn't really know what they did, but their business reach was drastically less widespread.

To her side, Hideo stretched out his arms and panned his head around, adopting the tone of one who clearly missed a chance to indulge his potential greatness. "I should've been an executive in the tech world. I really think I missed my calling."

Frowning, Dani looked doubtful. "Don't you need, like, ideas or entrepreneurial skills for that? Shouldn't you at least know something about the business world?"

As Hideo returned her sarcasm with a frown, Dani motioned to a splotch of ketchup on his lip—leftover from their recent fast-food meal, from one of those newer chains that prided itself on perfect burgers and nothing much else. "Or at least know something about grooming yourself?"

Annoyed, Hideo moved his finger to rub away the errant sauce. After removing the stain, he reassumed his thought experiment about missing out on tech greatness. "People like you are why it never happened. Nobody recognized my genius…or had the vision I possessed."

"Uh huh," replied Dani, looking around the parking lot for their contact.

"Truth is," continued Hideo. "You could have been my personal assistant. Made all my appointments… meetings… helped to facilitate my overthrow of the corporate powers that be."

Grinning, Dani faced toward the entrance to the main building. An untidy man, looking like he had lived at work for a week, made his way toward the detectives. Dave the security manager was dressed in a blue blazer and walked with the pace of one who was late for an appointment, either the one he now moved towards or several more that would likely follow their visit.

"Detectives?" asked Dave, using a voice that was distressed and overwhelmed. "Thanks for being on time. We have the video room ready for you. Sorry about being late, this place has been crazy since…it happened."

Stopping in front of Dani, Dave was apologetic and eager to please. His harried expression was made more pathetic by the intense worry that dominated his sad face.

Dani returned his gaze with a gracious smile. "Thank you for taking the time to meet us. It must be an awful time for your colleagues and company. Our condolences to everyone involved."

Dave stammered, as if he wanted to say more, but quickly fell into silence as he seemed at a loss for words. Nodding at him, Dani gestured with her arm for Dave to lead the way to the agreed meeting place.

As Dave spun around and paced back to the headquarters, Dani motioned for Hideo to precede her, giving her dreamy partner a servile nod as he walked past. "After you, Mr. Jobs."

#

Inside the CCTV and video room, the light was subdued. Lining the walls and a command area of comfortable seats—a place that held keyboards, buttons, and a large counter area—were a series of monitors, more than twenty in all.

Because of the low light and the 4K definition of the high-quality screens, as well as their individually huge sizes ranging in increments of between 43 and 65 inches, it was obvious a fortune had been spent to ensure every aspect of the property was observable and recordable by the equipment. Whoever had outfitted this security room had made sure that cost was not an object, and because this was the nerve center of Darby's empire, Dani suspected it was the CEO himself who had ordered the expensive setup.

Looking down and across the various banks of monitors, Dani was amazed at the detail and vantage points covered by the system. It appeared every possible point onto and inside the property was monitored to almost an absurd degree. A rabbit would find itself quickly seen if it tried to make entry to this private area, and that was only assuming it was able to scale the 8-foot solid fences that surrounded the company's property.

Dani was accustomed to looking at crappy images provided by banks and convenience stores, ones that often left you guessing about even the gender of the suspects involved, but here the razor-sharp and color images put everything else in her video experience to shame. Technology really had come a long way in the matter of camera and video clarity.

Impressed, Dani looked over at Dave, who nervously glanced around the dim room, visibly checking that the cameras and their viewpoints were properly aligned. Dani doubted his job as overseer of this place was long for this world, which would be the expected result when your head honcho gets murdered in a failure directly tied to security—or lack of it. Indeed, it wasn't often that any people kept their jobs in a clusterfuck of this magnitude, much less whoever was in charge.

Glancing sympathetically at Dave, she tried to sound not too harsh with her words. "I'm having a hard time seeing where the assailant came from. This great setup, and nobody knows…?"

Dave shook his head, equally baffled. "We don't get it either. We have time-stamped footage for the last month, with every inch of the exterior property line covered. It doesn't make any sense."

Frustrated, Dave reached down and tapped a keyboard, pressing the keys overly hard as he arranged something within the saved database. Pointing to the largest monitor on the wall, he was quiet as he waited for the saved file to open.

On that screen, a huge man, their undoubted killer, strode into a tree line, disappearing into a thicket of flowery bushes. This 5-second video loop was on auto-play, running over and over, making the scene sort of comical, like the attacker was a gargantuan clown exiting stage left.

Dani stifled the urge to laugh at the short clip, thinking that probably wouldn't go over well here. Gallows humor outside of police departments or morgues was not something you could usually count on.

The killer was unworried in his relaxed gait, which surprised Dani, but the most interesting point was his odd walk, like his huge frame wasn't quite constructed to move easily. Such a strange mode of movement was not something that would be easy to hide, along with a physical size that probably one in ten million men had. Near the end of the clip, the attacker lowered an axe from carrying it over his shoulder before stepping into the foliage, and the visible red substance covering the blade could only have been Darby's blood.

Dave finally spoke after Dani, Hideo, and a regular guard, perched on an out-of-the-way chair, watched it several times. "This is the only feed we have. The call from Mr. Darby indicated he was on the other side of the trail, and your department has geolocated that source to within a few feet. This video was taken after…"

As Dave's voice trailed off, Hideo took pity on the man and cleared his throat to distract Dave's anxiety. Gesturing to the entire array of screens monitoring the property's perimeter, he spoke the obvious. "Which can only mean he came from the inside."

Dave shook his head, and whatever his shortfalls at his job, he wasn't dumb enough to not notice a huge individual in the company, a person who would have quickly been arrested at this point. Whoever had done this must have come from inside, but it was evident the killer had yet to be identified.

Dani, still staring at the looping video, was intrigued about everything regarding the suspect: his size, his manner of walk, his weapon, and his choice of bizarre clothing, which made him look like one of those medieval role-players.

Breathing deep, Dani continued staring at the clip, letting her fascinated voice indicate her obvious surprise at the investigative situation. "So, we have a killer as large as 'Andre the Giant,' and no trace of him before or after the murder. And, of course, all of this happened in a high-security area under constant surveillance. Sound accurate?"

Confused looks came from everyone present, and nobody appeared willing to venture a guess about how this homicide could have happened, who could have done it, or indeed, why the CEO was chosen as the victim. Even Hideo, a smartass who made an art form of talking too much, was momentarily perplexed and silent.

Wrinkling her nose, Dani concentrated and placed her hands on the back of one of the chairs in front of the screens. She felt entirely clueless, and that was something that somehow excited her professional instincts.

Chapter Four

A rickety old sedan, a beige Ford Grenada of 1980s fame, pulled into an open parking space, with the number "17" barely visible in white paint on the curb in front of it. Around the space were wisps of grass and weeds that grew up from cracks in the asphalt road and concrete sidewalk.

The idling car faced a ramshackle apartment complex, one that had seen better days, even twenty years before the current time. Paint flaked from the sides of several greenish apartment buildings that were laid out in a haphazard fashion, and at various points in the chaotic parking area were several carports that seemed to cover only some of the vehicles at the facility.

Around the car were a few children on bikes, and the happy kids carried on with the business of having fun when left to their own devices. In these seedy surroundings, it was obviously a task they often got to do without adult supervision, but on the positive side, their laughs and carefree demeanor lent a pleasant atmosphere to the otherwise dreary residential area.

The sound of Hip-Hop boomed from somewhere deep within the complex, penetrating all the way inside Terry's dingy car. Turning off the engine, he looked around the inside of his ride, staring at a collection of McDonald's wrappers and cheap convenience store food containers scattered across the shabby passenger seat.

Holding up his phone, Terry took some time to look for something on the cheap mobile's screen. With a smile, he brought up a picture of a pretty woman, one that showed a somewhat surprised and dumbfounded lady, like she had not been expecting the photo to be taken. For a while, Terry stared at the strange image, his face assuming a wistful appearance, like this woman was the lost love of his life.

Catching himself, Terry frowned and put the phone away. Then, with a sigh and a creak from his car door, he hauled himself out of the vehicle and began walking to one of the buildings most distant from the parking area. Trudging across the parking lot, he held closely the paper bag containing his newly acquired figure, as if he thought someone might try to take the important item from him.

As Terry moved across the poorly landscaped grounds, it was apparent that a weed eater had not been used here for a long while, and garbage left unretrieved from overflowing trash receptacles made the complex seem even more tawdry. As he got nearer to his apartment, he frowned at the incessant thump of the music, which played from several buildings over and seemed intent on annoying as many random people as possible.

Terry had always had a hard time understanding why people blared their music in such a way. He was no big fan of any particular sort of music, with perhaps the exception of an occasional sampling of classic rock, but it didn't make much sense to him why you should intentionally irritate those around you with your favorite blasts of tunes. It wasn't like this was the only thing that puzzled Terry about residents in the area, but it was on the top of his list for being the most annoying and indecipherable trait of his low-income neighbors.

Coming up to his apartment door, Terry noticed that his mailbox near the entrance, the one that was bolted and locked like it held priceless valuables inside, was overflowing with junk mail jutting from the insertion slot. Frowning, he decided to leave the jumbled papers as they were, because any mail he did retrieve was likely to bring bills or other bad news he didn't currently feel like dealing with.

Jangling his keys, Terry unlocked the door and pushed it inwards. He was immediately surprised to hear the sound of the TV coming from inside. Sticking his head through the door, he looked hesitantly around the apartment's interior.

The apartment was somewhat tidy, with a large table in the eating area attached to the kitchen. The living room contained a simple couch and loveseat, along with a wooden coffee table arranged in front of a large-screen TV. On the walls were simple prints of famous paintings, with Andy Warhol being the most popular artist, inherited from the dusty frames of the apartment's prior residents.

Reclined and with a bottle of cheap beer propped in his lap, Terry's father, Wayne, stared at him from the weathered polyester couch. A substantial cloud of cigarette smoke hovered over him, and a well-used ashtray lay next to him on a couch cushion. In his late fifties and thin, the type of thin that made Iggy Pop seem positively obese, Wayne's rough features and negative attitude were accentuated by an unkempt beard and perpetual scowl. Shaking his head at Terry, Wayne showed his son a disapproving gaze as he motioned with a half-burned cigarette for him to shut the door.

Stepping inside and letting the door click shut, Terry looked at Wayne in confusion. His father should have been at work, but here he was, drinking beer and watching one of those fake courtroom programs that had people arguing over the stupidest matters imaginable. It wasn't a good sign to see him here at this early hour, and Terry tightened his panicked grip on the bag in his hand.

For several moments, they gazed at each other, with Terry periodically glancing at several more empty bottles on the table, while Wayne's unhidden grimace plumbed new depths of a negative mood towards his son.

"Dad…what are you doing home?" stammered Terry, trying to make it seem like a normal and non-judgmental question.

Wayne answered in a raspy voice, one that evidenced decades of his nicotine habit. "Uhh…just lost my job. Fuckers walked me out, and they didn't even let me get my cat."

"Cat?"

"Yeah," replied Wayne, obviously annoyed. "The warehouse where I worked, we had a stray we fed. Black and white one. The only thing I liked about that job. Fuckers."

"Was it just you?" asked Terry. "Did you…do something wrong?"

"Nah," answered Wayne, and he stabbed out his smoke and sat upright, his eyes alive with righteous anger. "They're just getting rid of us warehouse loaders. Always finding a way to screw the working man."

Silence followed for a time, and Terry cupped the half-orc figure in his hand, trying to keep his dad from seeing it.

Rubbing his hand over his scruffy face, Wayne polished off his drink and set the bottle aside. Standing with a grunt, he swaggered to the kitchen, where Terry had to get out of the way to let him by. Terry didn't make eye contact as his father leaned down to extract two more beers from the old and loudly humming refrigerator.

Setting the beers on the counter, Wayne opened both with an opener attached to one of the loops on his grimy jeans. Taking a long pull from one of the brews, he smacked in satisfaction and stifled a belch. Facing Terry, he displayed a look that bordered on revulsion.

"So, no more job," said Wayne, apparently not too disappointed by that fact. "Guess you'll have to pay the rent for a while."

More awkward silence followed. Looking down at the other beer, Terry, for the briefest of moments, had a surge of thirstiness. He was not one to drink very often, but he really couldn't remember a time when he and his dad had shared a drink. In fact, he couldn't recall a time they had shared anything, unless arguments could be counted.

"No…problem, I can cover it," Terry said, and he mentally moved around his insufficient income to come to terms with this new shortfall.

Wayne nodded, then returned to the couch—both beers in hand. Sitting down and kicking his legs up, he extracted another cigarette from a rumpled pack in his dirty button-down shirt. Taking his time, he lit it with an inexpensive red lighter while balancing both beer bottles between his legs.

Terry cleared his throat, sounding hopeful. "Dad…I'm gonna read my emails and maybe take a nap. Later, you wanna catch a movie? Maybe we can…"

Wayne shook his head and waved him off as he blew a new stream of smoke into the unventilated room. Pointing to Terry's hand-clenched bag and half-hidden figure, he spoke in a dismissive tone. "You still playin' with those toys? Playing Dragons 'n Dungeons…whatever you call that stupid shit?"

Like a chagrined toddler, Terry looked down at his feet. He didn't answer Wayne as he mulled over the hurtful words or intense shame that only his dad seemed able to evoke in him. A lifetime of contempt from his father had kept him in a more-or-less constant state of embarrassment, so at least Wayne was being consistent.

"Son, you're gonna have to grow up someday. Become a real man, instead of…"

Wayne shook his head as he trailed off. For a moment, he looked at Terry with the gaze of a parent that had only known disappointment and anger at the path his son had taken in life. Not one for introspection, Wayne didn't acknowledge his own role in shaping Terry's prospects.

Terry was well aware of his dad's feelings toward him, and the fact that his dad was himself an unemployed loser, giving up a job for the umpteenth time in the last several years, made Wayne's rebuke all the more painful. Brooding, Terry started to say something, then stopped.

Continuing to shake his head, Wayne lifted the remote and raised the volume on the argument in the reality courtroom. His gaze moved to the faces of strangers in that well-lit imitation of a place, and he quickly tuned out Terry entirely.

All the while, Terry fumbled with his unspoken words.

#

Pulling into a parking space in front of a brightly illuminated minimarket, Terry was in a pleasant mood. Around the entrance to the small grocery store, only a few pedestrians walked to and from its entrance, making for a quick prospective shopping experience. As he was in a hurry, that suited Terry's needs perfectly.

To the side of the entryway, a dirty homeless man sat in simple repose, leaning against the brick store wall and closely watching the few people that were out at this time of the warm day. Looking down, the man started counting a handful of change, but he stumbled through the effort, having to finally give up from poor vision and a lack of mathematical skills.

Inside his vehicle, Terry looked into the rearview mirror and took a moment to tamp down some stray hairs in his rather old-school bowl haircut. Taking a moment to focus into his own deep blue eyes, something that was really his only attractive physical trait, he smiled and tilted his head as if trying to gauge the effect his looks would have on a potential date. The closeness of the puffy reflection and his double chin made the effort unappealing, unfortunately.

Breathing deep from disappointment at his poor looks, Terry glanced to the side, taking note of several of his "Gamemaster" books, the uppermost of which read *Monster and Character Compendium*. In several folders and containers around the books were a mass of character sheets, maps, and background information on his created universe, along with several sets of dice and a plastic container containing his favorite painted figures. The frayed passenger seat was completely filled with the materials, items that he had spent years honing into a perfect role-playing universe for his games.

Leaving his car, Terry walked toward the small store, smiling respectfully at the homeless guy on the way in. When he was inside, he stopped for a moment, noticing an intriguing and somewhat familiar woman standing behind the cash register.

Emma was her name, and although some would consider her dumpy and unattractive, Terry always thought otherwise and tried to schedule his shopping visits to coincide with her work schedule. Glancing back at him, Emma seemed to be likewise interested, and Terry, never one to have ladies making that face at him, immediately blossomed into a deep blush.

Moving towards the back of the store, the place was typical for its various food and supplies, with aisles of overpriced treats and seemingly a hundred varieties of chips to choose from. Getting to the back of the mostly unoccupied store, Terry opened the cooler and withdrew several bottles of soda, as well as two twelve-packs of expensive canned beer.

Stumbling back to the front of the establishment, Terry lined up the drinks on the counter, then moved to grab several bags of chips to accompany the sodas and beer. As he carefully balanced them on the limited space of the counter, he met Emma's eyes, and again his face flushed red.

Emma looked back and nodded down at the materials. "Looks like you got a long night planned."

Hesitant, Terry continued his embarrassment, and because he was nervous, he didn't know what to do or say. Glancing around the store, he almost felt like Emma's interest was intended for someone else, yet he was the only one close enough for her to focus on.

Ringing up the items with several beeps from the register, Emma was nervous herself, and she spoke in a voice of hope and kindness. "That will be 35.50. Cash or credit?"

Fumbling out his wallet, Terry didn't answer, but instead counted out some crumpled bills and laid them next to her pretty hand. Continuing his descent into frazzled discomfort, he finished up the tally with a pocketful of change, and his hand nervously shook as he counted out the exact total.

As Emma moved the money into the till, they took turns meeting eyes and sharing mutual interest. For the moment, all other thoughts of his role-playing game or her boring shift were forgotten, such that a recently arrived customer behind Terry had to clear his throat for the transaction process to finally move on.

Snapping out of it, Emma took out a paper bag and started loading Terry's purchases into it. "Here…let me bag that for you."

Terry merely continued to smile, and after his items were packed, it took a while to take his eyes off Emma so he could leave the market. As he did so, he nodded his puppy-dog face in several quiet goodbyes, still too shy to say anything as he stumbled backward.

When he got to the front door, Terry continued to reverse-walk out the glass door. After he cleared the entrance, he ran straight into a huge man, one of the sort who munched on steroids and lifted weights by the thousands—in both repetitions and actual pounds.

In his thirties, Alex looked like a man that spent his whole life training his immense physique, and the results were impressive and intimidating. As Terry bounced off his house-like stature, Alex stared down at Terry's overweight and under-in-shape body, raising a lip in disgust, like Terry was something he had stepped in and would have to pick from the treads of his shoes.

Embarrassed, Terry nodded an apology for his clumsiness and tried to reassemble some of the chips that had fallen from his bag. As he did so, the bag ripped open, and his sodas cascaded down and rolled in several directions.

Alex continued to stare down at the overweight Terry, not offering to help him in any way, and instead gazed with an open-eyed stare, showing both deep disrespect and bullying intensity in his expression.

Terry took three trips to run down all his wayward snacks, moving them back to his car in batches as his shame and humiliation mounted. All the while, Alex continued to stand near the door and peer at him like he was a misshapen mutant. From inside, Emma noticed the scene and looked at Terry through the door with overt concern.

As Terry made his final trip to corral his food and drinks, he took his last bag of chips from the ground and handed it to the homeless man sitting to the side. The down-on-his-luck man nodded in appreciation and reached out a hand to shake. Terry took the offered hand and smiled worriedly before turning back to his weather-beaten car.

Jumping inside the vehicle, Terry put the car in reverse and backed out in a hurry, not taking any time to look again at either Alex or Emma. His vehicle, old and despite its engine's poor condition, accelerated rapidly into the late afternoon light, and Terry made his escape from yet another scene of personal embarrassment.

#

The exterior of the enormous house was beautiful, and prodigious solar lighting from expensive lamps ran the length of a tall brick wall encircling the property. In the middle of the home, a dome-like center hallway stood out against the night's dark skyline, while more lights highlighted the different and varied levels of the roofline around it.

A collection of windows of different sizes and placement looked out over a sea of manicured grass in the surrounding one-acre lot, providing easy views for the house's inhabitants. On the corners of the roofs, in easy view, were multiple security cameras watching the entirety of the property's well-defined perimeter.

The area in front of the structure contained a broad driveway, also lined with solar-powered lights that made it appear like a runaway due to its substantial size. An elegant garage faced the driveway with three separate doors sufficiently large to fit any vehicle of any size, and on the concrete-groomed approach to those doors, four vehicles were parked.

Three of the cars were expensive SUVs, in European flavors of Audi, Mercedes, and Land Rover, but the final vehicle in the assembled line was Terry's rust-challenged Ford. His humble car appeared out of place in the fancy environment, looking like a cheap hotdog planted in the middle of the finest food in a luxury meal.

Farther into the darkness, the quiet streets of the high-end neighborhood were completely silent at this time of night. The landscapers and workers that serviced the expensive and huge homes in this secluded area had long departed for the day, so only wealth and everything it bought filled the immaculate roads of the guarded Homeowners' Association.

Against the quiet night, loud rock music blared from the interior of this premium house. The tunes were straight from the 1980s, and though such music was out of place in the tony neighborhood, the beauty of living amongst money and privilege was that few people would question the personal preferences of enjoying oneself.

Inside the home, furnishings from the well-appointed living room and a kitchen, outfitted with exquisite marble and high-priced appliances, matched the expectations of the house's exterior. Three stainless steel ovens of different sizes faced an enormous kitchen island, while tiled floors reflected light across the interior with a bright and comfortable radiance.

Holding up Terry's half-orc figure, Jerome Sanders peered at the gaming piece with an intrigued stare. Fascinated, he held it up to the light, trying different viewing angles as he evaluated Terry's precise painting skill. The mini-figure seemed to look a bit different and stranger as he rotated it around, almost like it was a three-dimensional and almost-alive monster in his fingertips.

Watching from across the kitchen island, Terry waited for the judgment of his primary client. A few years older than Terry, Jerome was a successful and wealthy attorney. Even in this relaxed environment, he radiated a certain power as he continued his interested overview of the figure.

Jerome had a bald head that was diligently shaved and maintained, and that somehow sharpened his gaze and perceived intellect. Terry could never quite understand how bald men could sometimes look so much better than people like himself—those who had oodles of hair—but he nevertheless frowned, realizing that certainly was the case here.

As a ballad from Twisted Sister droned in the background, Terry waited in hopeful expectation, feeling like he was a student awaiting a final score on a term paper.

"Terry, my man, how do you do it?" asked Sanders, finally lowering the figure to the counter. "I've never seen anything quite like it."

Breathing out with relief, Terry smiled at the compliment and expectantly moved his gaze around the rest of the room.

To one side stood John Randall, who was of the same age and tax bracket as Jerome. With curly, still-blond hair and a smartass temperament, he smiled slyly at Terry as he swirled red wine in one of those enormous wine glasses, the type that somehow made the dark liquid inside look even tastier than normal. Just looking at the glass was making Terry thirsty, and he hated wine.

In the kitchen was Ben Jacobs, wearing glasses and also of the same age range. Looking into the window of a pricey microwave set into a bank of teak cabinets, he pressed several beeping buttons in an attempt to heat a sandwich inside. Looking on with bleary eyes and a swaying stature, he was having no luck figuring it out, and it appeared his meal would remain cold and uneaten for the moment.

"It's all about the motivation," said Terry, at last replying to Jerome's flattery. "They need to be perfect. I'm not religious, but it's almost like a faith with me. When I'm painting these things…I need perfection."

Randall arched an eyebrow, somehow managing to intensify his sarcastic stare at Terry. "Perfection? When you're painting little figures?"

Sanders rolled his eyes at Randall. "Dude, don't be a dick. He just likes to do it right. Society wouldn't be so fucked up if more people…"

Terry held up his hand, keeping his voice friendly and looking at Randall. "No, it's OK, Mr. Sanders. I'm not offended, and I'll try to explain. People go through life learning to do many things."

Terry pointed to Sanders. "Like becoming a successful attorney."

Sanders smiled back at Terry, appreciating the reference.

"Or owning a successful winery," Terry said, gesturing to Randall.

Randall grinned at Terry with an even bigger smile.

Terry motioned over to Jacobs, who was trying to pull the microwave out from the wall, as if getting at the wires in back would solve his sandwich problem. "Or even be a high-priced IT consultant, doing a job I never could understand, even after listening to the job description for hours on end."

Suddenly realizing he was the topic of conversation, Jacobs gave up on the frustrating appliance and peered back at the group with a sour expression.

"These are all cool things," continued Terry. "And I wish I could do 'em. But for me, I have to be the best in the world…at playing our game."

Terry motioned over to an expensive oak table that stood in an alcove next to the kitchen. With several bright lights above it, it lay next to a bay window that had an excellent view over the yard beyond it.

At the end of the table were all of Terry's books, stacked behind a screen that prevented players from seeing what the Dungeon Master was doing. Next to the books were character sheets and piles of various dice, from the triangular 4-sided all the way to the strangely shaped 20-sided variety.

In the middle of the table was a large mat, which was used for drawing maps, cave systems, and various buildings in the imaginary world. Made of a synthetic material, drawn items in the sword and magic universe could be erased and redrawn at will, allowing for a wide variety of gaming settings. Stacked in piles around the scribbled surface were several of Terry's figures, including brightly colored goblins, monks, undead zombies, and elves.

All these other figures were as realistic and striking as Terry's recently crafted half-orc. Pristine and immaculate, it was as if Michelangelo himself had been employed to make the characters as attractive as possible.

Filling out the rest of the surface area of the table were all manner of beers, wine glasses, and an almost-empty whiskey bottle. It appeared that a good bit of alcohol had been necessary to oil the wheels of enjoyment for the recently finished game.

"I get what you're saying," said Randall, but his eyes showed he neither got nor cared to understand Terry's singular focus on role-playing infamy. "And we've been with you for a long time, enjoying your 'work.'"

Sanders scowled again at Randall, giving him a firm *stop being an asshole* expression.

Randall continued, ignoring Sanders' silent pleas for kindness. "I just have to wonder if you put this effort into…well, anything else. Where would you be? You could still play the game as often as you wanted."

Frowning, Terry considered the suggestion, then shook his head. "I don't know, Mr. Randall. Honestly, I fail at everything else I do. Women. Career. Relationships."

A moment of silence followed, with Sanders and Randall sharing knowing glances at his admission, like each would have been surprised if Terry's situation was otherwise.

Stumbling from the kitchen, Jacobs broke into the conversation with slurred enthusiasm. "Ha, you're not alone there. Half the world can't do relationships…and the other half wishes they hadn't."

The mood livened somewhat, with everyone snickering at the interjection. All good humor had some truth at its core, and there was more than some in Jacobs' half-drunken assessment.

Letting his grin fade away, Randall leaned across the counter and looked Terry in the eye. "But we all live in REAL life. How would you feel if you followed perfection here, in the real world? Think of the things you could do."

Lowering his eyes, Terry was taken aback by the life advice, however well-intentioned or wise it was. Walking over to the table, he began packing his gaming supplies for the drive home.

The room was quiet as the others tried to figure out if he was offended.

"I think I'd be really depressed, Mr. Randall," said Terry, gently picking up his figures and placing them into a hard-sided container. "I need to be…who I am."

Looking apologetic, Sanders moved to the table as Terry completed his preparations for departure. Clapping their Dungeon Master on the shoulder, Sanders laid five crisp one-hundred-dollar bills in front of him. "Which is why we like you—and love your games. See you next Saturday, same time?"

Chapter Five

Birds chirped playfully in the waning light of day, providing a pleasant backdrop to the canvas painting. A diminutive hand, that of a dainty woman, moved near the canvas with a paintbrush. With the gentlest of efforts, the hand daubed some red hue onto the painting, making the dark and orange skyline perfect in the image.

From farther back, it was apparent the painting's intention was to be nearly a perfect copy of the real world. A remarkable rendition of the trees, brush, and grass in the forest and hills below was reflected in the painted portrayal of the natural scene.

The raw nature beyond the easel and its end-of-day sunlight was imitated in the artwork, done to a level of the best and most experienced artistry. Evening was arriving, and the created view in the painting was striking, matching the wildness of the panoramic setting to a substantial and impressive degree.

Sitting on a small chair, Carrie Flores looked at her efforts with a contented smile. Thirty-one years old and pretty, hers was the face that had been in the photo on Terry's phone, but her image had seemed younger on that mobile screen he had been admiring in his car.

Carrie continued to sit for some time and reflected on her work, as well as the beautiful scenery all around her. The truth was, she knew that life was a series of moments not often filled with peace and beauty, so she made it a point to always slow down and take in these times with appreciation for their briefness and poignancy.

In time, the sky began to drain of color, and the incoming darkness began to steal the gorgeous colors from the cloudless horizon. Breathing deep, Carrie understood her tranquil moment was ending, and she stood to stretch her lanky frame.

Behind her, her large SUV was parked with the back open. Sighing with disappointment, Carrie began to disassemble her things to go home. After breaking down her chair and painting palette, she lugged both toward the vehicle, making sure to not make a mess as she placed each into their reserved slots in the trunk compartment.

As Carrie returned to fetch her painting and stand, a different view, one from someone who watched her closely, came from fifty yards away. From that distance, the vantage point was from an elevated position in a tree looking down at her.

Staring and breathing with a wheeze, her watcher examined each movement of her loosely clothed outline with dark and probing eyes. As Carrie concluded her packing, the oddly hued night vision of her stalker focused on her bright body heat, and the breaths of the unseen stranger elevated in eager anticipation for what came next.

As if sensing the interloper, Carrie stopped what she was doing and looked around the isolated area. She knew that in such a remote place, she could only be alone, but a sudden and very real sense of danger began to prod her brain as her eyes scoured the abruptly foreboding surroundings. Not able to see or understand what she was looking for, she stood still for several torturous moments, holding her breath and scanning the woods.

Nothing. The area was apparently empty and harmless.

Relieved for the moment, Carrie quickly grabbed her painting and stand, returning to her vehicle in a rush. Not bothering to carefully place the things inside, she tossed them into the back, shut the trunk, and quickly made her way to the driver's side.

As Carrie clambered into the cab, her eyes again swept the area behind her, and she felt her attention drawn to where those strange eyes watched her. The copse of trees where the stranger was perched on a limb beckoned to her, as if that hidden figure called to her on some primal level.

As she locked her door, her heart pounded from her sudden and baffling exertions. Perplexed, Carrie felt like she had to escape from…something. Looking into her rearview mirror, she could see nothing to cause the anxiety, but her angst and worry did not decrease as she continued to stare; instead, they only increased over time, acting like a rising tsunami of fear and dread in her otherwise rational mind.

Starting the engine, Carrie stomped on the gas, throwing gravel from under the tires as the SUV accelerated into the descending night.

#

Ten minutes later, the high beams of Carrie's SUV illuminated a two-lane road that ran perpendicular to the dirt road she currently motored down. Slamming on her brakes, Carrie banked right onto the paved highway with a plume of dust spewing behind her. Ahead, the high beams of the substantial vehicle cut through the early night's shadows, acting like probing undersea cones of brightness as she barreled through the rural area's encroaching darkness.

Looking back to where she exited the dirt road, Carrie's panicked eyes expected something to shoot from between the trees in pursuit of her. The horrible dread of being chased seemed to grow worse by the moment, and for the first time in her life, Carrie knew what a hunted rabbit must feel like as it tried to evade the clutches of some unseen and utterly terrifying predator.

Fortunately, as Carrie sped down the highway, nothing moved out to follow her, and when she turned left on a long arc in the narrow road, there was no pursuer visible behind her.

Still, her alarm and sense of something horribly wrong did not recede. A feeling of wanton trepidation coursed through her bones, forcing her to constantly scan in front, to the side, and directly behind the speeding vehicle.

She could feel something out there, something that was not of this world, looming just at the perimeter of everything she knew as logical. She couldn't quite put a finger on it, but she knew its origin was otherworldly, or at least unknowable. *What the fuck is going on?*

Carrie had always prided herself on science, or as she referred to it, the "glorious scientific method." She knew that one didn't need to be a scientist to follow the tenets of adhering to provable phenomena, either in their own lives or by observing the world at large. Science didn't rely on beliefs to exist, it simply relied on provable facts.

This meant that for everything, there was a cause. If a tree fell, it was because it was cut down, or its roots were too weak, or a hurricane blew it over, or any of one thousand other reasons that brought about a result. If it happened to fall on some poor soul on a trip to the woods, that was entirely mournful and sad, but it also just meant that poor schlub was in the wrong place at the wrong time. It wasn't that he was cursed or hadn't spoken the right prayer, it was just that his statistical chance at his life ending had been fulfilled prematurely, which was something that happened all the time, across all countries and times.

It was the same way with lottery winners, which was the undoubtedly worst form of gambling in God's existence—if He was indeed there. Someone who won five hundred million dollars on a ticket matching random numbers they had chosen from life's various numbers must feel like a lucky, fortunate, and blessed person, but in reality, it was statistically impossible at some point for someone not to win. The fact was that good fortune was ordained to happen to somebody.

Yes, something coherent and explainable caused other things to happen, and all the mumbo jumbo in the world people embraced to make the world seem mysterious and meaningful was utter bullshit; life was entirely about scientific principles of causation and repeatable experimentation.

And yet, here was Carrie driving thirty miles over the speed limit on a remote road, fleeing something she neither saw nor sensed with her five senses. Glancing again in the rearview mirror, she smiled without humor at the irony of it all, but she still kept the speed of her vehicle pegged at a velocity that was decidedly more dangerous than the boogeyman she had imagined in her worried mind. *Calm down. You're gonna wrap yourself around a tree.*

After ten more minutes, her pulse had returned to a degree of normalcy. Up ahead, the highway merged to the right, and there it flowed onto a divided freeway, one that had two lanes going in each direction. Far in the distance were the lights of

Sacramento, the capital of California, and ground zero for her normal and very mundane life. She breathed a sigh of relief.

Over time, the road grew wider still, and the illumination from yet more lights made the way forward ever brighter. Looking less in her mirror, Carrie decided she must be having hormonal changes of some variety that were driving her crazy. She had been keeping up on her birth control, but the thought that she might be one of the small percentage who failed with her pill did creep into her mind. Frowning, she understood if that was the case, at least her husband Carlos would be happy with the failure of science to prevent it.

Exiting the freeway, she pointed her vehicle towards one of the endless apartment complexes that circled the city. They had the good fortune to live in a good area, so although Carrie loved her forays into the countryside for her opportunities to paint, she was glad to see the familiar streets and stores near their humble condominium. She did know one thing, though: *I'm never going back again to that fucking canyon.*

Pulling into their reserved parking space, she nodded approvingly at the sign that stated, "Sunny Estates." Safe and sound, Carrie decided on the spot that she wouldn't be watching horror movies for a few days. Around her SUV, knots of people went about their business, walking amongst the extensive park area and trees that abutted their orderly complex.

Like a medicine that has a "rebound" and suddenly causes symptoms it is supposed to treat to get worse, Carrie's guts suddenly knotted into a more pronounced version of the dread she had recently experienced. Almost leaning over from her anxiety, she scanned the pleasant area for anything that could endanger her. The feeling of impending doom was overwhelming, like she was swimming in an endless dark sea laced with piercing physical horror and existential fear.

Only a few couples walked near her building, taking casual strolls in the early night. Nothing else seemed out of place, and she could even see their condo door from where she parked. Reaching into her purse, she felt for her .38 revolver, a five-shot version that her husband made her keep and get a concealed-carry permit for.

"You can never be too safe around here, even when you think it's totally secure," he'd said. *How right he was. In fact, I think I'm going to the toilet with it for the rest of my life.*

Thumbing the cylinder open, Carrie checked to ensure it was filled with cartridges, and she exhaled a sigh of relief when she realized it was fully loaded. Focusing carefully ahead, she exited the vehicle and strode bravely toward her front door.

Slowing down, she moved haltingly towards a bend in the trail that would lead to her brown wooden entryway. Her eyes scanned the attractive area, looking for something she knew was out there, something that was evil and unstoppable. Something she absolutely felt wanted to destroy her on some sick and vindictive level.

Turning down the long concrete path leading to her door, each step forward was a triumph of her will over her want to flee in fear. Ever the one to laugh at the unknown, Carrie was now like a scared girl as she pleaded in her mind for the safe harbor of her home. Pacing slowly, she collected her courage to overcome her terror, but she also knew she would no longer be a proponent of the blind skepticism that so dominated most of her adult life.

Stopping her walk, something else crossed Carrie's mind, and she mulled a new issue over. She suddenly knew something else because of this brush with…whatever it was. This external force, which made its presence known in such a penetrating and loathsome manner, which was grinding her nerves in such an evil and abrasive way, meant something else to her life: it meant there was indeed evil in the world, but what of the opposite? If an external and supernatural force could so destroy her notions of safety and well-being, then the opposite must be true as well.

Rational thought meant many things to assorted people, but if you rationally agreed that there were very bad things in the world, and not just the type of bad that people did to each other all the time, but instead a detached and sentient malevolence that existed in this material world—like she now experienced—then you must also admit that good is similarly present, and it must also have a cause, something that compels structures and individuals throughout society to act for the benefit of others—to offer choices for the betterment of yourself and your community.

Uncomfortably, Carrie realized such a conception of a good and external presence sounded very much like the "God" that all the religious folks focused their lives around. She had never been hostile to such people, but she also had never given anything they had to say any credence. Gradually she realized that may now have to change, at least if she survived her encounter with the horrid thing she felt was so near.

Restarting her walk, Carrie advanced toward her precious home, which lay right ahead, beckoning her with its homeyness and simplicity. She was not an overly sentimental sort of person, she felt people leaning on love and other pleasant emotions too much often cheapened the very thing they liked about them, but at that moment, the view of her modest residence seemed like the gates of heaven itself.

Behind some thick trees on the side of her path forward, that same unnatural night vision from the canyon focused on her slow-walking feet from behind an extensive hedge running between their building and the next. As Carrie got closer to her door, the viewpoint of the short figure moved closer to her condo's entrance, staying out of her peripheral vision as it edged nearer.

In seconds, Carrie's bizarre stalker would be there, ready to leap upon her as she opened the door. Creeping forward, it placed itself in a perfect position to be within easy striking distance when the time came.

"How ya doing, gorgeous?" said Carlos, approaching from the other direction.

Wearing the uniform of a deputy from Sacramento County, Carrie's husband emerged from a path that ran the length in front of their apartment structure. At the far end of the sidewalk was his police cruiser, which was parked in an emergency-only area across the exit point of the apartment complex's main pedestrian pathway.

Turning to see Carlos, Carrie was surprised but relieved. "Carlos, I…uh…didn't know you were coming home early."

Stepping close to her, Carlos pecked her on the cheek and held up a plastic bag. The food's aroma was dreamy. "I'm not; I just got some takeout, those subs you love from Tantinos. Figured you might like some company for dinner. Um…something wrong?"

With a loving and thankful smile, Carrie thought for a second, then shook her head and motioned to their condo's door. All her worries and distress melted away with the kind presence and affable smile of her husband. The horrible feeling that plagued her dissipated as suddenly as it had appeared.

As their diminutive observer backed away from the couple and retreated into the dim shadows of nearby foliage, she sunk her key into the door's brawny lock.

Chapter Six

Terry looked eager and determined as he stared down at his desk in the dim reception area. He licked his lips in anticipation of what came next, letting the ecstasy of the upcoming goodness bathe his senses in an expectant and anticipatory moment.

Reaching down, Terry grabbed a slice of the double cheese and meat pizza laid out before him. Holding it up, he gnawed on the edge of the gooey mess, inclining his head so as to allow the flimsy crust sufficient room to droop as he pulled it into his mouth.

Terry's eyes watered as he slathered the cheesy food down his throat, and for a moment, he understood the perfection of what was the sublime and ultimate food: pizza. He imagined that the Italians had invented the stuff; at some time or another, he had heard of their pioneering work with his favorite grub, but he also knew that it took American ingenuity to construct what he was now consuming.

Most countries in the world could and had invented some tasty cuisine, but only in America could you then stack four kinds of meat on it, fill the crust with yet more spongy cheese, and then see to it that everyone in society saw the bloated result as the pinnacle of savory greatness.

Pulling too hard on the slice, the sea of toppings slid from the top of the slice and tumbled down his shirt, interrupting Terry's moment of stark happiness.

"Shit," exclaimed Terry, hopping up from his seat and patting at his uniform shirt in surprise. The resultant streak of grease and sauce on his wrinkled button-down shirt left a horrible stain on the security uniform.

Terry was standing in the middle of a lobby, one that was like countless others that housed worker drones throughout the state and country. Shiny walls of polished tiles surrounded him, but because of the need to save on energy, only a few lights currently illuminated the shadowy area.

A bank of clean windows was in front of Terry, and looking through them showed a courtyard and street in the pale night outside. No sounds or anything to watch presented themselves at the moment, and the result was something like perfection for anyone wishing to be left alone to pursue personal interests—and somehow get paid for it.

As Terry picked at the stain on his uniform, he frowned at his name tag, which showed "Brandt" at a crooked angle across the breast. The shoulder of the frayed shirt displayed a patch that read "Security," but in truth, it just announced to the world that *I have a pulse, so they hired me.*

Frustrated, Terry moved to his chair and retrieved his coat. Pulling on the old and tattered jacket, one that was given away for free from a gaming convention, he was just able to hide the incriminating pizza stain from the surrounding world.

From the glass door at the front of the lobby came a tapping on the window, and a surprised Terry squinted to overcome the reflection and see who was paying him a visit. Moving forward with a disappointed frown, he stepped within feet of the glass to see what lay beyond.

When visibility sharpened enough, Dani and Hideo came into view. Looking at Terry with inquiring eyes and fake smiles, they each held up detective shields and pointed pleasantly toward the entrance.

Terry's frown deepened considerably as he ran his hand over the patchy stubble on his soft jowls, and curiosity and worry filled his expression as he met their eyes through the glass barrier. Nodding, he moved toward the door as he pulled a set of jingling keys from his pocket.

#

A couple of minutes later, Terry stood by his security desk, his eyes uncomfortable and his bearing awkward. Obviously unhappy with his guests, he took turns sneaking glances at them while avoiding any prolonged eye contact.

Dani and Hideo stood near him, their faces held in a common and unnerving smile. It was an amusing aspect to these sorts of interactions that everyone present knew there was no honesty or genuine respect to be had in the upcoming questions, but on the police side—at least for the moment—they always sought to uphold a facade of politeness.

Smacking a mouth full of gum, Hideo smiled even brighter at Terry, like they were the oldest and best of friends. Terry returned the look with a concerned scowl, not biting at the gesture of faux friendship.

Pursing her lips, Dani stood with a thick folder in her hands. Her gaze took in the whole lobby, as well as Terry and his disheveled appearance. She even frowned at the large pizza stain on his shirt, which Terry's cheap jacket now failed to completely cover.

"What can I do for you, detectives?" Terry finally asked, his voice low and insincere. "It's the middle of the night."

"Don't worry about that, Mr. Brandt," replied Hideo, continuing his gum-smacking with a knowing grin. "We checked with your bosses. Made sure it's OK to visit you."

Getting a visit from the police at your job was not the best career-enhancing situation when working in security. Terry knew this, and more importantly, so did Dani and Hideo, meaning Hideo's humored look became infuriating as he continued his calculating smile at the rotund security guard.

Terry bit down the urge to voice his frustration at the police presence in his long-cherished and very quiet workplace. Biting his lip and affecting a certain nonchalance, he acted surprised at them turning up here. "I don't get many visitors here. Especially cops."

Moving close to Terry's desk, Dani took notice of a gaggle of his play figures arranged on the surface near the pizza box. They were the same Terry had used at Sanders' house, where he had held his last game, and he made a habit of taking them to his overnight job.

"You may have heard about the murder at the Technology Center, Mr. Brandt?" asked Dani, moving her eyes methodically to focus on Terry. "The CEO of an investment company was killed…in a very strange way. It was quite a horrific scene."

"I…think so," said Terry, avoiding Dani's stare. "It's been on the news, but I'm not usually up on current events."

"Really?" responded Dani. "Because this particular CEO—Reginald Darby—was someone of direct interest to you. I had imagined you knew about him in some detail, including where he worked."

"Yep," added Hideo, joining the conversation. "It could be that not only you knew him, but you also made a habit of making threats regarding his company's business."

Terry answered them with a confused stare, like his interrogators were speaking an entirely different language.

Terry may have been a lowly security guard, but Dani thought his acting skills were well above average. Maybe he even missed his calling in Hollywood.

Sighing, she took a paper from her folder and slapped it next to the figures on the desk. "This is an email from you to Mr. Darby. In it, you call him a 'rat-bastard shithead,' which I think is pretty creative, and tell him, 'You'll get yours, eventually.'"

Terry's jaw hardened as he avoided Dani's glare and looked out the window. Staying quiet, he apparently had nothing to say.

Shrugging, Dani took more sheets out of her folder, laying them next to the last. These were screen shots of social media posts, and several of the sentences were circled in Dani's red pen.

Motioning to the papers, Dani continued. "And from your social media accounts. Here, you describe him as 'heartless,' 'predatory,' and 'scum…who needs to reap what he has sewn.' All of this because he runs an investment firm?"

Slowly, Terry's eyes moved to Dani. In his gaze, she saw two things she hadn't expected: defiance and simmering rage. At that moment, she knew he had to be her man. She didn't know the how or even the specific why of the crime, but boiling rage like she now witnessed was all she needed to know about the direction the case would take. That's what her intuition and senses told her, and she had learned to trust them long ago.

Terry gestured down to the pages, speaking with quivering resentment. "That 'investment firm' buys companies, fires people…destroys lives. It's not fair. It's never fair with these kinds of people. They use workers and throw them away like garbage when they're no longer good for the bottom line."

Stepping closer to Terry, Hideo nodded, doing his best impression of *Workers Unite* with a mock-raised fist. "Perhaps he did these things, Mr. Brandt. Maybe he was a cruel and bad person. Betcha think that was a good reason to take revenge? Fix the problem?"

Stepping closer from the other side, partially surrounding Terry, Dani spoke in a soft voice. "And it's worse that Mr. Darby was in the process of buying your father's company, right? Seems like yet another reason for some payback, even if it was before your father was fired?"

Nodding with that continued playful grin, Hideo looked expectantly at Terry, testing the boundaries of the guard's self-control.

There was silence for a time as Terry visibly contained his emotions. Composing himself, he met the suspicious stares of both Dani and Hideo. "I was here the night of Darby's death. I'd never hurt anyone, even a worthless human being like that."

Spinning around, Hideo took two steps away before turning back again and staring at Terry. Crossing his arms, he raised an eyebrow, evincing a Sherlock-Holmes expression—one that would have been comical if not for the serious subject. "It seems, contrary to what you said, you really are 'up on current events.' Your view of the business world would make Che Guevara proud, and you've somehow managed to arrange for an alibi during this crazy killing?"

Terry stared back at Hideo, then let his gaze wander to the door in a sign of wanting them both to leave. Apparently, he was unwilling to elaborate further on his views.

Dani answered in Terry's place, smiling wryly. "Yes, you were here. We've already seen your company's CCTV footage for that night. Still…when I see threats meet reality, I really have to wonder. I've never believed in coincidences when they involve murder, even when a worthless human being is involved."

Taking a long breath, Terry stayed quiet. His former frustration and anger faded away, replaced by a controlled and unreadable expression.

Glancing back to his desk, Dani focused on Terry's figures again. With an amused expression, she plucked up the Half-Orc fighter and held it up to the limited light. "What's this? A warrior? I played D&D when I was a kid, but I've never seen something this good. Love the realistic detail and…nice axe."

Setting down her folder, Dani used her free hand to touch the small edge of the Orc's axe with her fingertip, as if she sought to evaluate the real-world cutting edge of the miniscule weapon. Annoyed, Terry suddenly reached for his figure, but Dani held it away with mischievous eyes.

"Can I borrow this for a few days?" asked Dani, keeping an innocent smile. "I'd like to try to copy your style. I never could figure out how to paint—."

"No," interjected Terry, raising his voice. "I really need to get back to work. I got nothing else to say to you guys, and I'm not who you're looking for."

Trading a glance with Hideo, Dani thought for a moment. When she spoke, her expression was clinical and calm, like everything she had just witnessed was expected and foreseen. "Fair enough, Terry. We'll be in touch…if…WHEN we need to chat more."

Before handing the little monster figure back to Terry, Dani took her phone out and photographed the figure. Before turning for the door, she did the same with the other characters on the desk below.

Silently, Dani and Hideo exited the building. When they were gone, Terry locked the door behind them with a clack of the metal and glass door.

Returning his gaze to his desk and food, Terry chewed on his lip, thinking hard as he considered the detectives and their not-very-subtle accusations. Looking at his now-cooled pizza, he realized the cheese wouldn't taste nearly as good now.

Chapter Seven

The courtroom was almost empty at the end of the day, and only a few stragglers stood around the confines of the room's clean, wood-paneled interior. To the back of the room, near the area where a judge usually oversaw proceedings in both civil and criminal matters, a young female stenographer packed up her stenotype machine, while varied observers of the recently out-for-the-day court case quietly filed from the entrance in an orderly manner.

At one of the counselor's tables, an early middle-aged woman looked down at her notes as she leaned over her mixed paperwork. Marjorie, dressed smartly and frowning, looked the part of an attorney who knew her business, as well as the constraints and frustrations of the profession she'd chosen. After finishing up with a few notes, her expression soured as she began to put away books, papers, and electronic gadgets— things that were the tools of her always-challenging job.

Completing her day's work, Marjorie faced the entrance to the courtroom and was pleased to see she would be the last to depart the public area. Today's results sucked, but she always realized the best way to succeed in anything, be it as a lawyer, a salesperson, owning your own restaurant, or whatever, was to outwork and pay attention to the small details that surround you.

To overcome your opponent meant to make the minutia of your work as important as the larger picture. She couldn't count the times she witnessed the success of a case hinging on a detail that many self-important and well-paid lawyers had missed before her.

Marjorie knew that if you were always looking to be the first one out the door or to rest because your day was somehow overwhelming, there would, in turn, be someone who would be happy to take away your advantage or livelihood. The weak and lazy would be weeded out or delegated to a poor living by their actions, and that was just the way of the world; there was nothing personal about it, it was simply like pronouncing the answer to an easy math problem—it was what it was. It wasn't that her position made her think she was a better person or necessarily smarter, she merely understood that hard and diligent work carried you farther in life, whatever job you chose.

Sighing, Marjorie smiled at the irony of her current predicament, because despite her pursuit of effectively performing her job and watching the details of her work with manic care, she faced a very different outcome than what had originally been envisioned.

Sliding a carrying satchel around her neck to face backwards, she hefted a briefcase in her strong hand and made her way out of the now-empty room. As she exited the doorway, her eyes caught on the seal of California adorning the immaculate wall, and somehow, she was briefly saddened by the image, like it was a brand moniker of her profession that had absolutely nothing to do with success, reality, or rightness.

In the hallway outside, a young and pretty woman quickly came to Marjorie's side. Claire, just out of law school and bathed in makeup, rushed up to her with exasperated features. The younger woman had not yet figured out that sometimes less is more, and her overuse of eyeshadow and prodigious lipstick made her appear a bit like an older version of a cupie doll.

"That didn't go as planned," said Claire, lifting her own bag over her shoulder as she looked hesitantly at her boss.

Marjorie shook her head in agreement, motioning down the long marble hallway for them to walk. Claire fell in beside her as their high-heel shoes clicked in concert on the hard surface.

"No," replied Marjorie, pursing her lips beneath her attractive features, ones that were properly maintained and exuded the perfect balance between recognizing her age and still ensuring her appearance was enhanced with proper feminine accents. "It certainly did not."

"I never saw an expert witness contradict…our own case," said Claire. "Why exactly are we paying him?"

Marjorie frowned as she kept a smooth pace down the hallway. "Because we chose badly. This 'slam dunk' just became a debacle."

"What are we going to do?" asked Claire, her voice rising. "We can't win—."

"The first thing we do is calm down," replied Marjorie, looking over with a firm smile and a moderate tone, one with a gentle warning just under the surface. "Histrionics do nothing for us—or the client."

Claire nodded at the gentle rejoinder, working to keep up with Marjorie. Despite her youth and similar height, she was one step behind as the professional women walked on.

Coming near the wide front door to the courthouse, Marjorie glanced at several of the security personnel who guarded the main entrance. Descending from their vantage point out the majestic entryway of the building were a series of wide concrete steps, with the result that the area looked somewhat like an ancient Roman Amphitheater in front of the imposing structure.

Marjorie stopped and faced Claire, who pulled up next to her with a confused look. Marjorie kept her voice low, speaking in a way that suggested she was imparting some great wisdom to the youthful employee.

"Claire, are you a sports fan?"

Staying quiet, Claire shook her head.

"In any sport, you can come to a point when a single play shows you who is going to win the game," said Marjorie, and she watched the few last stragglers pass out of the building's control point. "It might be in the first quarter, with three-fourths of the game left, but you know at that point what the result will be. Now, this doesn't happen often, but a smart woman knows when to recognize that moment when it stares her in the face. Men often don't get that, because they let their egos get in the way of common sense. Especially smart men."

Claire considered this for a moment, going through the possibilities in her worried mind. "We can still petition—."

"That play just happened," Marjorie said, talking over her subordinate. "The game is over; the rest is just a matter of semantics."

"There's still the testimony of…" Claire offered, but her face became dejected as her words drifted off, lost in Marjorie's stern shake of the head.

Leaning closer, Marjorie tried to keep her voice pleasant, even as the icy precision of her stare showed no inclination towards happiness. Business was business, and it was time to play the hand they had screwed up so spectacularly. "Call the client. STRONGLY recommend they settle. If this goes to the jury, those hicks are going to horse-fuck their company, and rightly so. Along with our reputation."

Silence came in response as Claire processed where they were at. Stunned, she pulled out her phone and stared wistfully down at it. "I…thought we had them dead-to-rights."

Marjorie shrugged, showing a weathered and sincere smile. "Yes, so did I. But…we can live to fight another day. And…bill another hour."

Turning away, Marjorie left her young assistant to do the dirty work of surrendering. She knew you couldn't win them all, but the act of raising the professional white flag was something she could never quite stomach.

#

Two hours later, Marjorie stood on the sidewalk next to a nearby restaurant. Having finished some other work over nachos and a margarita, she was now under a sky that poured sheets of driving water, filling the streets and sidewalks with vast and undulating puddles.

Holding up an umbrella, Marjorie seemed unperturbed by the deluge around her. With her briefcase in one hand and the shield of the expensive umbrella above her, she looked positively calm. Meanwhile, less-prepared and soaked pedestrians sprinted by in search of refuge from the storm's onslaught all around her.

Watching the diverse people hurrying around, Marjorie smiled at the funny appearance of individuals dressed in light shirts and blouses as they frantically tried to avoid the water that drenched them so thoroughly. It was obvious to Marjorie that the discomfort they felt was entirely preventable because, although they didn't need to spend almost a thousand dollars on the Burberry umbrella she possessed, anyone with a brain could have consulted a simple app on their phone to discover that thunderstorms were expected in the late afternoon.

Marjorie wondered what it was about humanity that people rarely made rational decisions regarding their behavior. Some people smoked like chimneys and died a painful death at forty because of it, while others raced on motorcycles through traffic to often end up as road pizza underneath a truck or splattered against a tree or light pole.

It wasn't that there weren't smokers who lived long, Marjorie had read that the oldest woman who ever lived smoked until she was 117 years old, but in reality, there was plentiful information to dissuade people from making bad decisions—easily available online, and not hard to find in almost any language.

Likewise, many motorbike riders lived long and enjoyable lives, but nevertheless, Marjorie personally knew several people that died violent deaths because of their love of speed and using their crotch-rockets of choice.

Moreover, to stretch Marjorie's internal point further, everyone knew what professions paid the most, and it wasn't hard to figure out what it took to become a doctor, an engineer, an IT specialist, etc. So why did people continually enroll in universities to pursue studies that had little chance of offering a prosperous career when the world was full of jobs and specialties, from plumbers to cooks, that could lead to an enjoyable life where there was plenty of need? Smirking, she thought about a neighbor down the street who retired at forty-five because he was a welder and made insane amounts of money over the previous twenty years in pipeline work. Statistically, he would live a long and relaxing life because he made a rational and profitable choice of employment.

In the long past, society did not have access to widespread and accurate information, so at least individuals could be forgiven due to their ignorance of negative outcomes. But now it appeared that the more information that was available, the dumber people got.

How long had the medical community known about the detrimental effects of obesity, and still, American waistlines grew continuously outward? Even as little as a couple decades ago, when Marjorie labored in law school and sustained herself on noodles, it was rare to see young people overweight, but now it appeared half the teenage population jostled about with horrendously mushy physiques.

Back to her immediate surroundings, Marjorie grinned some more and thought that it served them right, all these scrambling people around her, to be getting soaked. After all, what did at least one of those small and cheap umbrellas cost? *Fifteen dollars, maybe twenty?*

As she waited for her ride, Marjorie grew positively happy at her own wisdom regarding these matters, conveniently forgetting about the fifteen extra pounds of weight she herself carried or the drinks after work that were such a staple of her everyday life. Addictions and bad outcomes were only a problem for other people, it seemed.

Suddenly, Marjorie was pushed forward, and she almost stumbled into the street from the unexpected impact. Catching her balance, she righted herself and cast an annoyed glance behind at the funny-dressed man who accidentally ran into her. Ducking into a crowd of pedestrians that flowed down the sidewalk, the man, covered in an odd leather overcoat, melted into the sea of busy after-work humanity pressing against one another.

Irritated, Marjorie turned back to the street, where she was then happy to see her ride-share SUV pull up. She always preferred the premium rides available with the app, and she was happy to see, in this case, a large and spacious Volvo with plenty of elbowroom to spread out inside. Pulling open the door, she looked over to see a Hindi-looking driver with an immense and expectant smile on his face.

Scooting into her seat, Marjorie grinned at the man and spoke with some enthusiasm. "418 Montclair Court. Take your time; there's no hurry."

As the driver nodded and turned his attention to the downpour splattering against the windshield, Marjorie leaned back to enjoy the ride.

#

Marjorie's ride pulled close to the curb in the affluent area. Overhead, the rain had, for the moment, stopped, leaving a sheen of the water that covered everything around the pleasant neighborhood. Down the street, the community full of custom homes and individually crafted landscaping stretched into the distance under the overcast sky.

The air was crisp from the pleasant aroma of recent rain, made more so by the wide selection of well-tended flowering plants in various gardens along the walkways in the exclusive housing development. Nothing was quite like rainwater and lush flowers to enliven and make an environment acutely refreshing, and Marjorie grinned at the extensive and attractive yards lining the street around the idling SUV.

After paying her still-smiling driver, Marjorie stepped from the clean back seat to a clean concrete pathway stretching toward her house. Glancing back at the man, she thought for a moment about his pleasant demeanor. She was always amazed how some people just had that striking capacity to be nice and endearing to everyone around, no matter the weather or state of their lives, either emotionally or financially. Whatever that guy took to keep that perma-smile going, she would gladly pay good money to get the same results on a consistent basis.

Stretching herself, Marjorie focused on that enormous door that offered entry to her private world at the end of a long stretch of personal walkway. To either side of the path were a multitude of colorful plants and trimmed hedges, but inside her house was the place she most loved to shut herself off from the world.

Her inner sanctum was her home, a place of relatively spartan surroundings, but nevertheless a cherished setting she loved more than anything. Always single, she never could get used to the thought of accepting another person into it, either in the form of a lover or a roommate, and each day she came home was a time for her to unwind and enjoy the area that was her own, without worries, partners or legalese to intrude on its beautiful and cultured simplicity.

Moving closer to the expensive entry door, the beautiful dark oak one that had cost her a fortune in time and money to have installed, Marjorie's heels clicked boisterously against the firm and crack-free pavement below.

As Marjorie moved closer to her home, she stumbled a bit and was confused by the errant placement of one of her feet. Below, it suddenly seemed a little more difficult to ensure the placement of each step forward, and she found herself obsessing as she used precise pressure in every leg movement to walk normally. Haltingly, she realized her muscles weren't working properly, and each lunge ahead was off-kilter, like her limbs were being operated by someone else.

Halfway to her goal, it seemed that the door had not moved any closer; indeed, it looked almost as if the intervening space had yawned farther yet, and Marjorie had strangely made no progress at all. In her chest, she felt a pain that sharpened inside the organs of her upper body, making her formerly pleasant feeling fall away and forcing her to squint as she tried to understand what was going on.

Confused, Marjorie began to feel unfocused, and it was almost like she was floating above her own body, like that time she had stupidly taken hallucinogens with her friends from the sorority at her university. Try as she might, she couldn't avoid the feeling of everything not feeling in its place, even as she approached the most loved of all destinations in her daily life.

She stumbled closer to her home, but oddly, it no longer held the allure it had moments before. Stopping, she tried to shake away this peculiar feeling, running her tongue over her lips as she moved her baffled gaze around her front yard. An odd monotone gurgle crept up her throat, a horrific sound that frightened her, but she worriedly felt herself unable to control it.

Taking two more steps, Marjorie was within feet of her door, but it was a place that still seemed a lifetime of distance away. Leaning down, she tried to collect herself and dodge this crazy fugue that made her world seem so strange at present. *Get…yourself…together.*

Feeling a sharp and overpowering pain in her chest, it also felt like her limbs had become dead weight. Her head suddenly was numb, and as agony swept down her torso and throughout the rest of her body, she knew something was dreadfully amiss. Trying to pan her head about, hoping to look for someone who might help her in this traumatic moment, she swooned and then collapsed onto the wet pavement below.

Marjorie's face cracked brutally against that hard surface, and worse, she made no effort to stop her fall. Sprawled in a heap on the soaked pavement, one arm was turned up, while her right leg convulsed at an odd angle to the side of her heaped form.

Taking her final breaths, her now-blue lips quivered while half her face was immersed in a puddle of rainwater near the approach to her gorgeous house. As the light went out in her distressed mind, she briefly wondered why the end had to come in such an undignified fashion, just a small distance from where she had long expected to peacefully pass away several decades later.

Chapter Eight

Subdued light from several streetlamps cast a pleasant glow throughout the park. The sounds of playing children mixed with distant music across the evening's descending shadows, and crowds of happy families were enjoying themselves at the scattered picnic tables and smoking barbecues of the public area.

On an extended field to the side, several teens and children threw frisbees and played soccer, while at the end of the field, groups of mixed-age people enjoyed a loud game of badminton across a drooping net. Throughout the genial environment were shouts of competitive challenges and hopeful encouragement as the assorted teams and individuals warred for a chance at weekend-sports infamy.

All told, the friendly vibe of the relaxing and communal atmosphere made the scene attractive and lively, as if it was an advertisement for the joys of family life and domestic bliss.

Emma sat alone at the end of one of the tables, staring out over the assorted family units that were enjoying the moment. She had a look of reservation on her face, like she was waiting for an invite to be part of this extended group.

Emma scowled a bit at the children and couples that smiled and played, wondering what it would take to eventually have her place in such a world. She realized it was not something you could easily plan to make real, and you just had to wait for your turn to have a husband and children.

All of her past romantic mistakes had occurred precisely because Emma was too eager for this surrounding result, so now she was going to play it cool and make certain she chose wisely. Getting what you wanted in life meant being more careful with your decisions, but before today she had never been wise enough to choose a partner that was good for her life's goals. She decided that would have to change, starting now.

Dressed in a simple and attractive dress, Emma straightened out the frown on her face and affected a look to show the world she was happy in her singleness. It may have been awkward for anyone that cared to look, but it was important for her own sense of self-worth that she be happy with her station in life—at least somewhat, anyway.

"Hi…I'm glad you came," said Terry, looking at her from a grassy area behind her. Dressed in a tucked-in white shirt that was perhaps too tight, he waved reservedly at Emma. Having walked on a jogging path from the other direction she was facing, Emma had not seen him approach, and for a moment, surprise flashed over her face.

Catching herself, Emma smiled bashfully. She was glad to see Terry, and she ran her hand through her recently curled-and-cleaned dark hair. Wearing makeup that made her plain features more attractive than usual, she had obviously made some effort to spruce herself up for the late-evening date. She motioned with a grin for him to sit across from her, trying to seem relaxed as she met his eyes.

Terry held out a plastic bag of Chinese food, placing it on the concrete table before sitting down. "They had a special tonight on the orange chicken, so I got extra. When it's two-for-one, you can make out like a bandit."

Opening the bag of food, Terry began to remove the containers of steaming rice and meat, arranging them for their meal. Extracting plastic forks, knives, and paper plates, he dutifully laid them in front of Emma and followed up with some napkins.

Chuckling, Emma nodded at the food, then motioned to the area around them. "You're a real gourmet and a high roller. It…was a cool idea to come here for dinner."

"I figured I had to find something different for a girl like you," said Terry, blushing. "Because you're so pretty and all."

Emma's face brightened at the compliment, and her own flush of red indicated some embarrassment. "You're just saying that, right? I get asked out like…never. Aren't many princes left in the world. For me, at least."

Letting her gaze drift to the side, Emma stared wistfully at a mixed-race couple sitting on a patch of grass and having a picnic. The mom and dad were each playing with one of their beautiful twin daughters, with smiles and affectionate giggles filling the young toddlers' faces as they made ecstatic and indecipherable talk with their adoring parents.

"I've never said anything more honest or true in my whole life," Terry said, and his features became serious. "I think you're beautiful."

Looking back at Terry, Emma considered his tone, like she was gauging his words and thoughts. After several moments of indecision, she decided he wasn't being sarcastic.

Silence continued for a long time as Terry returned her stare. He kept his focus on her, like she was the only thing he wanted to see or pay attention to in the busy area. For once in a long time, Emma felt like she was the center of attention in somebody else's world.

Terry's endearing stare was honest and intense, and it made Emma feel special as she continued her evaluation of Terry's motives. It was always difficult to know what you were facing when on a first date, but the first indications of attraction and interest were positive signs. Sometimes she agreed with the notion that "all the good ones are taken," but she was also open to being convinced otherwise. *If at first you don't succeed, keep fucking trying.*

Letting a genuine grin fill her face, Emma leaned closer to get a better look at the delicious-smelling takeout food.

#

Two hours later, most of the park was now empty. In the nearby field, there were now only two remaining children kicking a soccer ball, and around the rest of the picnic area were just a few people cleaning up and packing their unfinished food.

In a line of woods, where the jogging path ducked into several stands of trees towards the inner part of the park, a few walkers and late-night exercise freaks exercised under the strong glare of a continuous set of light posts. With few remaining people around, the public area was now devoid of loud voices or music.

Walking out of the community park, Terry strolled at the side of Emma. Trying to look kind and interested, he kept his gaze on her as they exited the area.

"So, my ex decided he wanted men instead," said Emma, clearly embarrassed at the revelation, both because she had been dumped by yet another guy and because of the jokes she often got from acquaintances about converting the man away from heterosexuality. "I really couldn't figure out how to compete with that."

Snickering, Terry got ready to reply, but seeing her eyes go wide in potential anger, he held up his hands to placate her. "Uhh…I wasn't laughing at you. It's just…I never got far enough in a relationship to get dumped like that. In a way, you've been a big success…compared to me."

Thinking it over, Emma shrugged as they continued their after-meal jaunt. After leaving the park, they merged onto the sidewalk of a quiet street in a modest development of single-story houses. The streetlights were less robust here, and the stretches of road ahead were shrouded in splotchy darkness.

"Well, life goes on," said Emma. "Not like I can change the past. God, if I could though, I would've run away from that bastard."

They fell into silence as they strolled through the neighborhood of quiet homes and curbs packed with cheap cars. The intermittent blare of televisions from living rooms only a few yards off the street showed the tight-packed conditions of houses built close to the street, a common facet of dense developments from this 1970s-built area.

Looking ahead, Emma mentally waved away her regrets of the recent past. Letting her depressed tone die away, she tried to sound cheery as she changed the subject. "What do you like to do for fun? You into sports? UFC or boxing? I love watching fighting."

Looking surprised by the question, Terry tilted his head and gazed down the street. He lowered his voice as he mumbled an unenthusiastic response. "Uhh…not really."

Oblivious to Terry's reluctance to answer, Emma continued. "What do you like, then? What do you do for fun?"

Emma's words were clear, but Terry took some time to answer, clearly terrified about disclosing his primary hobby. "I…like to umm…play games."

Emma nodded eagerly. "Like video games? That's cool, 'cuz I do the same. It's a blast wasting other people online. I usually play the US side in World War Two shooters. Lots of girls don't like to, but—."

"Not those types," Terry said, gently interrupting. "The kind where you pretend you're in a different world and use magic. Go on quests and kill monsters…it's kinda like video games—without the graphics."

"You mean…Dungeons and…Dragons…with those books? Like in grade school, when…?"

Terry's face grew mortified, like he had just been exposed as a pedophile in prison. Looking around, it appeared for a moment he might actually run into the night, screaming in fear and never to be seen again. If he was in any decent shape, he might well have done just that, but he instead opted for an uncomfortable silence.

Fortunately, Emma wasn't fazed by the revelation. "Ahh, don't get offended. Everyone's got their thing. It's a bit strange—but not too weird. You should have seen what my last boyfriend wanted me to do with his…"

Emma stopped that thought, realizing a bit too late it wasn't something most people would want to hear about, especially a prospective partner. Keeping her pleasant disposition, she chewed on her lip as she considered how best to restart their conversation.

Terry got happier when she was quiet, quickly realizing his hobby wouldn't mean the end of their date. With many women, it would have, but in truth, with many women, there wouldn't haven't been a date in the first place.

"You don't think it disqualifies me?" asked Terry. "Makes me any less sexy?"

To accentuate his question, Terry shot Emma a "Mr. Olympia pose," where he flexed his pudgy frame in mock ridicule of his own poor physical shape.

Emma laughed at the self-deprecating move, putting a hand on his shoulder as they stared at each other on the sidewalk. Leaving her hand there for some time, they continued to lock eyes, enjoying the solidarity of their less-than-perfect physiques and looks.

Emma thought for a moment, then smiled up at Terry. "I think the world is full of abusers…meth freaks…and liars. If playing kids' games is the worst thing you do, I'll be just fine with that."

Chapter Nine

Hideo stared out the windshield of the unmarked police cruiser, watching the lights of scattered urban stores and apartment buildings flash by. It was night outside, but the steady stream of illumination from city lampposts and bulletin-board advertisements made visibility easy.

Reaching down, Hideo extracFted a handful of pork rinds from a plastic bag and stuffed them into his mouth. As he chewed noisily, Dani stared over at him from the passenger seat. She had a perplexed look on her face, the one that was both intrigued and disgusted at the same time, like she was a gawker peering at the remnants of a fatal car accident. She gazed at Hideo for several moments, interested yet revolted.

"How do you eat those nasty pork rinds?" asked Dani, fighting the urge to be ill. "You know they're just deep-fried pig skin? They taste like spicy, Styrofoam ass."

Hideo shrugged and added yet more of the morsels to his mouth from the rapidly depleting bag. Choosing not to answer, he crunched louder and took the time to loudly lick his fingers clean of the seasoning that coated his hand. Dani looked away to avoid a gag response.

For a minute, they were both quiet, with Dani struggling to avoid being annoyed as Hideo continued his impromptu meal. Letting her mind wander, Dani looked out the window to take in the suburban strip malls and improving neighborhoods as the vehicle sped ahead.

Dani could never figure out why she ended up doing this kind of work. Raised in a middle-class home in New Mexico, she had a fondness for desert sunsets and beer, neither of which offered an easy means of making a living. After college, she had migrated to California in pursuit of a boyfriend that offered to make a home for them here, promising love eternal.

Unfortunately, that man, Chris was his name, had a love for beer and California sunsets that far exceeded her own, and worse yet, he found another companion to watch them with, frittering away his free time with a woman named Svetlana. That he had met some sleek Slavic package was bad enough, but he neglected to let Dani know she was no longer the sole benefit of his affection, and long before their relationship actually ended, he was getting his sunsets from two directions at once.

When Dani had packed to leave their cheap apartment, she still remembered the crappy feeling of knowing she had been used for years on end, sort of like a toy that a kid played with and threw away when bored from the monotonous fun it provided. He hadn't even had the temerity to see her off when she left, instead hiding in his room and watching *The Price is Right*. She still hated that fucking show, no matter who it was that replaced the old dude running it before.

Such thoughts really made Dani appreciate the benefits and sometimes joy of remaining single. Sure, occasionally it would have been nice to hang out with someone as the years flitted by, but that was why God invented cats. There was no hassle and no drama with felines, and even though Dani knew cats were the least loyal creatures on earth, you could at least lock them in your house until they eventually had to be nice to you. True, she had never actually adopted one, but she had many years of being a spinster before that truly became necessary.

After the clusterfuck of the breakup, Dani had seen an ad for the police, a place she could put her degree and a talent for obsessing over small things to good use. After a few years, she had moved from patrol all the way up to detective, which allowed her to focus on cases in absolute detail until they were solved. Every time, she solved her case, no matter how many weekends or holidays of her own time it took to pursue them.

Dani found the best part of police work was that it was pretty easy to solve things, as long as you were willing to put the time in to make it happen. Other detectives wanted to have barbecues and spend time with family on their days off, but with Dani not having to worry about a cheating partner, she did a lot of her best work in the confines of her small home.

Dani supposed, in time, she could have gone elsewhere and really moved up the law enforcement ladder, perhaps working for the state or finding some cushy job at a corporate security office, but this now felt to her like the best job in the world, where she got to put her OCD to work for the good of other people. Of course, she didn't do it for other people—if she was to be open with herself—but at least it made her feel good to know that sometimes actual people were helped by her law-inspired exploits.

Returning to the present, Dani moved her attention to her own hand, where she tried to make the "Spock" greeting by holding her fingers in a "V" position. Long intrigued by the *Star Trek* universe, she could never quite master the muscle control to make the sign properly.

Crinkling up his empty bag, Hideo took notice of her movements. "I never knew you were a gaming geek. You're also a 'Trekkie'?"

Dani looked over at him with a condescending grin. "You just figured out why I'm single? Men can't handle a woman that speaks fluent Klingon."

Hideo chuckled, incredulous and amused. "You go to those conventions, too? Dress up and pay a hundred bucks for Sulu's autograph?"

Lowering her voice, Dani took on a sultry tone. "I dress up in a Romulan bikini. I find I make more friends that way."

Hideo laughed again, grinning at the thought. But, a slight blush also colored his face, showing the bikini image was not one he would necessarily dislike, if he was to be honest. Of course, such honesty wouldn't be forthcoming any time soon in their entirely professional relationship.

Pointing up ahead, Dani motioned to a street on the right, where several police lights flashed across a series of homes that stood behind a gated housing development. "Take a right there. Looks like half the force beat us here."

#

The dark street near Marjorie's house was filled with the strobes of several police cars, creating a checkered fluorescent montage on the neighborhood's buildings. A small crowd of locals, all with concerned stares and sad expressions, stood near two lengths of yellow police tape, staring worriedly at the entrance of their neighbor's residence in the exclusive and normally drama-free development.

Mumbling apologies and stepping through the assembled crowd, Dani made her way to the front of the closed-off sidewalk. Walking close behind her, Hideo held a notepad and somehow managed to scrawl in it despite the darkness and quiet chaos surrounding him.

Flashing her detective's badge to a disinterested cop, Dani stepped under the makeshift barrier and paced toward the house. On the path near the entrance of the home was the sprawled and unmoving form of Marjorie, who had almost made it all the way to her treasured home.

Standing above the dead woman was Officer Hendricks, in his forties and bald as smooth granite. Marjorie had been turned over at some point, and her lifeless face shined a pasty reflection under the beam of Hendrick's flashlight. Leaning so close that he almost looked to be trying to kiss her, Hendricks examined her face with some intensity, as if he soon expected her to talk to him.

"Hendricks, what are you doing?" asked Dani, raising her voice in annoyance.

Looking up from the corpse, Hendricks played his light across Dani's face, then over to Hideo's likewise-irritated features. "Dani, what are you doing here? We got an aneurysm here—or maybe a heart attack. Not a homicide."

Stepping closer, Dani lowered her voice and pointed to the side at a group of chatting officers and civilians, people who must have avoided the police barrier to get a closer look. "Could be, Hendricks. But the thing is, I get to determine that. Would you mind clearing those people away?"

Hendricks was kind enough to keep illuminating Dani's face with his bright flashlight, letting it linger on her irked expression for a few moments longer. With a huff, he shut off the beam and moved toward the too-close crowd of onlookers.

Looking over to Hideo, Dani nodded to him and leaned down over the still form of Marjorie. Taking out a penlight, Dani moved a gloved hand over the bruise on the woman's face, poking at the yellowish dead flesh of a hideous bruise. Grimacing, she stared directly into the deceased lawyer's vacant pupils.

Glancing down at Dani, Hideo continued writing in his notepad. Shaking his head, he motioned back toward Hendricks, who was ushering the group of cops and curious neighbors back to the street. "He could be right. People drop dead all the time."

Continuing to lean over Marjorie, Dani ran her hands through the decedent's pockets while holding the small light in her mouth. Pulling herself fully erect, she nodded in agreement and took the light from between her teeth. "Yeah, no doubt. But do you know who this is?"

"Should I?"

"It's Marjorie Bettencourt," replied Dani, talking as if the information was privileged. "Senior partner at the law firm of Bettencourt and Associates."

"I'm waiting for the punch line."

Dani made a vague motion to the south, towards the far-off corporate park. "A firm that's on retainer to Benelux Capital—one of their biggest clients, in fact. Handles their mergers and acquisitions."

Nodding, Hideo resumed writing. "So, you think this has something to do with the axe-murder? Thought you were bird-dogging that loser security guard on that?"

Not responding, Dani rolled the body over with a grunt. Jostling the corpse, she ran her hands up under her coat, like she was feeling the woman up. Searching for something, she performed a thorough pat down of the almost-cold body as she looked for any sign of violence or indication of foul play. Sighing, Dani steadied herself and came to her full height. She appeared confused and looked back towards the road as she pondered what happened.

The right eye of the lawyer had showed some kind of rupture, with blood pooling in streaks from whatever happened inside her head. Dani had seen and dealt with many victims of such a death, and it looked like a burst vessel in her brain could certainly be a tragic cause of her demise. Dealing with corpses for a living had a way of making her immune to the human side of things, and this woman's life had ended in such a seemingly sad way that she could use her developed coldness to brush this under the rug of solved and natural deaths.

But there was something else to this as well. Dani had heard the call about the dead lady and immediately recognized the name from a background workup she had been doing on the murder of Reginald Darby. It shocked her to hear of the early death of Darby's attorney. Indeed, it surprised her so much that her inner voice had screamed at her to grab Hideo and come to examine the body before the coroner took it away.

Something was terribly wrong here, and it felt like bullshit to call it the normal course of things.

The problem was, a woman in her late forties and in apparent decent health rarely dropped dead. Death found everyone on its own terms, but that was almost always in a bed at the hospital, in hospice, or in the case of a junky, face down on dirty concrete with veins full of some noxious substance or other. It wasn't common for decedents to expire randomly unless they were on the toilet or involved in some other blood-pressure-raising venture. Walking up their sidewalk after work had a calming effect, and Dani had never heard of someone keeling over at such a moment.

The fact that it was someone connected to her other victim made the occurrence even more strange and noteworthy. Unusual events happened in isolation, but they almost never occurred in chains of abnormal circumstances, especially when a killing was involved. As much as it would be easy for Dani to just clap her hands together and wash away this new death in a torrent of paperwork, it didn't feel right. Something clawed inside Dani's brain, forcing its way into her consciousness, like a bull clambering its way into a peaceful church. *What the hell am I missing?*

"So, nobody can die who knew the other victim?" Hideo asked, interrupting her thoughts. "Could be a coincidence, right?"

Chewing on her lip, Dani thought for a moment longer. Ignoring Hideo, she leaned down, running her fingers through the dead lawyer's hair and massaging the scalp, almost like she was washing it in preparation for a haircut.

After a moment, Dani gently laid Marjorie's lulling head back down to the concrete. Holding up her hand, she shone her light on the tight fingertip of her glove, where a drop of blood was smeared on the white plastic. Peeling off the glove, she withdrew an evidence bag from her pocket and dropped it inside.

Glancing back to Hideo, Dani held out the bag for him to take. "A person who dies of a stroke or heart attack doesn't have a little hole in their scalp that seems to be a puncture mark. Especially on the back of her head, when she fell on their face."

Hideo took the bag, raising his eyebrows in an impressed expression. "Which means…?"

"We have another murder," said Dani, showing a practiced grimace. "Find out where this lady was, what she was doing, and who she was with. Everything. This situation just got more complicated, and it might get a lot worse."

Chapter Ten

As the squeaky door was pushed open, pale light from the outside's overcast sky flooded into the darkened room. The shadowy insides of the dingy bar were revealed in all its glory, with various drunks slumped at intermittent spots throughout the place, nursing their drinks with sunken and bloodshot eyes.

Along the wall were several black-and-white framed photos of a man in a white T-shirt, a strapping fellow who smiled alongside various muscle cars in a sign of better times—both for him and the establishment his pictures now hung in. In the attached room that stretched to the back of the bar, where the painted red walls were full of yet more nostalgic photographs, a single unoccupied, scuffed pool table awaited players in the faint light.

As the door to the gloomy establishment shut, Ted, the bartender, looked up from his perch behind the bar. Well into his fifties, his dulled eyes and rosy cheeks showed a person perhaps too fond of his own stock of alcohol. Though he was too young to be the man in all the car shows from the past, his too-large nose and similar sturdy jawline made clear his genetic connection to the man in those images.

Wayne surveyed the bar for a while, standing near the now-closed door and staring at the sad men who made this place their daytime haunt. These despairing drunks' faces, sorrowful in the best of times, combined with the low lighting and made their demeanors even more pathetic than even their low station in life might have indicated.

But, these sad individuals were also Wayne's type of people, and something like an enthusiastic grin crossed his face as he moved toward his normal place on a corner barstool. He nodded pleasantly at several compatriots in drink as he shuffled to that spot.

"How ya doin', Ted?" Wayne asked, trying to be polite as he seated himself on the creaking stool. "Whiskey, please."

Stepping close to Wayne, Ted lowered his voice and shook his head. He spoke in a gravelly voice, a throaty one that evidenced a man who had inhaled enough smoke, either from his own cigarette habit or through prodigious secondhand exposure, to overwhelm his shriveled vocal cords. "You gotta pay your tab, Wayne. This ain't no charity—I got bills, too."

Wayne shrugged innocently. "I lost my job. I'll catch up when the unemployment starts. It always takes forever to kick in."

Doubtful, Ted grimaced in response. "You were late payin', even when you were working."

With no verbal reply, Wayne looked back with imploring eyes. He let a grin tug at the corner of his own mouth, alluding to the camaraderie of the drunken club they were both so deeply a part of, a club that allowed for someone to float you until the next paycheck.

Frowning, Ted considered the sob story, which was one he had heard many times over the years. Running a bar well in a local setting meant having to extend lines of credit to your clientele in consideration of the ups and downs they endured, and Wayne was certainly a high-quality customer in that regard.

After shaking his head, Ted reached back and grabbed a bottle from a shelf full of various cheap brands. Setting a half-dirty glass in front of Wayne, he poured a generous portion as Wayne stared expectantly. Shaking his head, Ted moved back to a dark corner near a sink, where he picked up a dirty rag and absently cleaned a beer mug.

Taking a deep breath, Wayne looked down at his treasured liquor. Now was his time, the time to saddle up and change his perspective for a while. Everything would seem right for a time here in a place he could forget his troubles and disappointments. He might even have some agreeable conversation with some of the regulars, people that thought about the world just like he did. It was always a great feeling to be around like-minded folks, even if that like-mindedness came from a bottle and the buzz it induced.

Gently grabbing the whiskey glass, Wayne got ready to enjoy his workday.

#

Later, Wayne sat at his same spot near the tawdry wood-grained bar, crisscrossed as it was with faintly carved initials and long-unnamable stains. Cradling his drink, he stared ahead and watched himself in the dark mirror running behind racks of liquor bottles in back of the bar. With an unshaven face and deep circles above his sagging cheeks, he realized he wasn't going to win any beauty contests in the near future.

Shaking his head, Wayne reached over and grabbed a handful of peanuts, which were likely to be his only food for a while. Munching on the stale and salty food, he nursed his whiskey, knowing he had to prolong the moment in order to truly enjoy it. Part of appreciating the bar life was not only getting accustomed to the low light, delirious companionship, and the distant sound of country music, but also truly living in the moment. Wayne was a connoisseur of this lifestyle; it was, in fact, one of the only things he had ever relished in his miserable time on earth.

Around Wayne, the bar's other customers had drifted away, and only he was currently resident. The monotonous hum of a crooning singer, bemoaning the loss of a long-lost love and coming from elevated speakers on the wall, was the only sound to keep him company.

From behind Wayne, the door opened, and diminished evening light flooded in to illuminate the dour surroundings. He paid it no attention, instead focusing his bleary eyes on one of his aged and wrinkled hands as he popped a few more peanuts into his mouth.

Terry stepped next to his father at the bar. Looking worriedly over, he spoke in a concerned voice. "Dad? Thought I'd come and check on you. Wanted to make sure you're OK."

Glancing over, Wayne acknowledged Terry with a grunt. Motioning to Ted, who was enmeshed in reading a bikini-and-sports-car magazine, Wayne slurred his words. "Get one for my son. Would ya?"

"I'll have a Diet Coke, please," said Terry, sounding out of place. "In a can—no glass."

As Ted retrieved his drink, Terry settled into the stool next to his father. Raising his voice, he spoke tentatively. "I called the distributor, Capitol Foods, over in the warehouse district. They said they got plenty of work."

"More work," replied Wayne. "One thing there always is, is more work."

"They told me to have you come down. Said they can get you going next week."

Facing sideways, Wayne fixed his son with an irritated stare. "Did ya know, son, that the work never ends? No matter what ya do? No matter how hard ya try?"

Looking sad, Terry nodded in agreement. "I know, Dad. It isn't right, and it doesn't seem like it will ever change. Always someone taking advantage of the little guy."

Wayne snorted agreement, then quaffed the last splash of his drink. Grimacing at the heavenly taste, he raised his voice. "Ya know, when your mom left, I thought, 'the hell with her.' I thought we could do without the cheatin' bitch."

Terry's eyes teared up at the mention of his mom, and he glanced over at Ted, who acted deaf to the discussion. Ted had undoubtedly heard and would hear a thousand more talks like this, but he was a seasoned professional at playing dumb to overheard conversations.

Wayne continued in his droning bout of self-pity. "I thought maybe I could get ahead in this world without her. But…it didn't happen. And here we are."

Wayne stumbled to his feet and leaned against the bar. Pointedly, he avoided looking at Terry. "And I wonder what I gotta do now. To make it. Other guys got their kids to take care 'em. But me…I got nothing."

Shaking his head and grumbling to himself, Wayne stumbled past Terry and made his way to the bathroom, bumping into tables and chairs on the way. As he moved off, Terry's chin quivered at the unhidden insult.

After several moments, Terry collected himself. Looking at Ted, he nodded towards the bathroom and tried to hide his shame. "I'll take him home. What's he owe?"

Ted responded in that raspy voice, sounding reluctant as he peered at Terry. "Three hundred will cover today—and his running tab. From last month."

Sighing, Terry pulled out his wallet. Staring into its confines, he frowned at the too-few bills inside. "Will you take a check?"

#

The cluttered bedroom was darkish, except for scattered light filtering through the long back window from a lamppost outside. Around the window were grimy and tattered curtains, so old they must have served several prior inhabitants in this oft-rented apartment. The walls of the small room were covered in cheap glossy paint, the sort that inhibited stains from children's scribbles or other common causes of wear and tear.

Terry stood in the doorway in the vague light, looking down at his dozing father. Wayne snored peacefully on his twin bed, passed out and apparently in good shape to retire for the night. His feet jutted awkwardly over the end of the bed, with his heavy leather boots making it seem he had reclined for a short rest in the middle of a workday.

Frowning, Terry moved to lay a heavy blanket over his dad, taking his time to ensure it adequately covered him for an extended sleep. Moving to Wayne's feet, it took some time for him to untie and remove Wayne's old work boots, then orderly set them to the side. Taking his time, Terry even arranged the laces to line up in a presentable manner for the next time his father was ready to go out.

Rummaging around the rest of the bedroom, Terry picked up several discarded items of clothing, placing them into a large laundry basket. As he did so, he grimaced, holding the dirty items away from his body with two fingers, like they might infect him with some uncontrolled bacteria.

Next, Terry moved to the top of Wayne's dresser, where a host of beer bottles had been left empty for several days. Setting them atop the clothing, he backed out of the bedroom with his arms full. After shutting the door with his foot, he angled to the front room, where he set down the laundry near the door for a future trip to the laundromat.

Continuing his cleaning efforts, Terry moved about the front room and kitchen to fetch still more bottles of empty booze, sweeping them into a trash receptacle with a disgusted shrug. Shaking his head, he wasn't pleased with once again being the only one who cared that they lived like pigs.

Terry loved his dad, but he didn't understand him. It seemed to Terry that his father only lived to drink, and he didn't care for anything or anyone else. He knew that many would consider Wayne an alcoholic, but that word didn't hold the same meaning for Terry as it did for the rest of society.

Terry had been around drinking and drunkenness his entire childhood. While he himself didn't often indulge in an alcoholic beverage, it was such a regular part of his existence that it was normal to see its results in everyday life. What he didn't like, however, was the collection of garbage afterwards—smelly bottles and cans of the half-empty stuff lying around.

For some reason, this messy background after the fact was far worse than the act of constant inebriation and its attached downside of nonsensical blather and sometimes violence that drunk people often engaged in. Such People usually came to their senses after sobering up and often were rational afterwards, but the garbage they left behind was somehow sickening to him. In his own mind, Terry knew there must be a psychological reason behind this peculiar revulsion he felt to booze garbage, but he wasn't concerned with the cause, just the affect.

Moving to the kitchen table, Terry bagged up the last of the refuse and set it aside with a distasteful scowl. Collecting his thoughts, he moved to sit at the end of the table, where several of his books and miniature figures were arranged. As he sat down, he focused on his set of game pieces with a suddenly determined and anticipatory face.

Grabbing a book with the same title *Monster and Character Compendium*, Terry set it gently before himself, arranging the hefty tome like it was a cherished bible from antiquity.

Reaching over, Terry picked up one of his play figures and moved it to the top of the book.

Crafted and painted to a high standard, the figure looked like a character from a Kung Fu film, with a bald head and controlled expression on its tiny emotionless face. It wore flowing brown robes and was in a fierce fighting stance, giving the impression it was ready to attack at a moment's notice.

A smile crossed Terry's face, and his eyes went wide expectantly. Moving his head on a swivel to loosen his neck, Terry peered down at the play figure and took several deeper breaths. Staring for a period of several minutes, his face went slack, and his features became absent, as if he was no longer mentally present in the room.

As more time passed, a sheen of sweat formed across Terry's face, beading up on his forehead and upper lip, despite the rather chilly temperature in the frigidly air-conditioned apartment. In spite of his detached gaze, a distant and odd smile began to form on his eager features.

Chapter Eleven

The front of the store was lit by descending light from the waning afternoon, as well as numerous light posts running along the strip mall's extensive sidewalk. Most of the customers for the day had moved on to other venues, and what remained were people jostling with bags of groceries as they moved to their cars from a trendy organic food store that stood to the side of the gaming establishment.

Inside the comic store, it was nearly empty at the end of the day, with only a single fourteen-year-old boy lingering near a rack of magazines and books in the back of the place. Elsewhere, the lights had already been turned out in aisles of board games and assorted fake weapons, such as plastic maces and mock medieval armor.

Above the young man, an awkward boy who was overweight and pimply, was a cardboard sign that read

"Witchcraft." The writing was surrounded with poorly painted blue stars to invoke a sense of the magical, but the result just showed a horrible sense of style from the artist. The teen anxiously perused a magazine that had dragons on its cover, and his eyes danced across the page, reading an engrossing story of warriors and wizards fighting a horde of undead monsters.

"Gotta close up shop," said Badger, reluctantly interrupting the reading. "The missus awaits."

Upset, the boy looked dejected, like he wanted to stay all night. Not meeting Badger's gaze, he put the magazine back into a rack of similar titles. Speaking in a squeaky voice, his anxiety at losing his hangout for the day was palpable. "OK, sorry…I stayed too long. Just like always."

Badger responded to the teen with a magnanimous smile. Leaning close, he kept his tone cheery and pointed to a row of old books that lined the far back wall. The various used and tattered books faced outward, cover-first, and looked mysterious in the faint light. "No worries. If you come back tomorrow, I'll show you some real magic. MONDO magic."

The boy's face brightened, and his excitement was rekindled for another upcoming day of geek happiness. Suddenly enthusiastic, the young man paced toward the front of the store with a grinning Badger trailing after him. All was well for the moment in the life of the young and nerdy.

Graciously letting the teen out, Badger waved goodbye and reversed the sign to indicate the store was now closed. Clicking the lock into place, he was contented with his place in life, and he moved to the cash register to close out the books for the day.

Looking back to the door, Badger thought for a moment about the clumsiness of growing up and loving this world of imagination and far-fetched entertainment. It was difficult enough as a young man to adjust to the brutal world they all lived in, and he now saw himself in that ungainly boy, several decades removed.

Badger remembered his own time in his early teens, with exciting conventions and nights spent with gaming friends over pizza and sodas, often playing over books until the wee hours of the morning. He remembered character sheets and vicious battles with demons and vampires, where they often managed to survive the most perilous fights as they battled to overcome terrifying monsters of every variety.

Strangely, those get-togethers spent with long-forgotten friends stuck out in his memory more than any trips with family or sporting events that were often the fondest recollections of other boys. In fact, the irony of having such wonderful memories of fake adventures, as opposed to the real world of quality time spent in real-world endeavors, was lost on him. The life of the role-playing gamer was not for everyone, and it required a certain amount of apathy towards others, especially family, as you grew up.

Besides, glancing around, Badger now had assembled a bit of an empire from his love of such gaming, and he took in his surroundings with beaming pride. It was all his doing, and who gets to have a life like this, doing what they truly love? *If there's a heaven on earth, I've found it.*

Looking down at his old-style cash register, Badger pushed a button on the till and was rewarded with a unique ding as it popped open, revealing rows of dirty cash collected from the pockets of anxious kids—and not a few adults, as older folks also loved to indulge their juvenile joys later in life.

A tapping from the front door tore Badger from his thoughts, and he looked out through the opaque glass to see two figures standing there. Unable to recognize the identities of the dark shapes, he kept his merry outlook and approached the entrance.

Unlocking the door, he swung it wide and spoke in an apologetic tone. "Sorry, closed for the night. Please come back…"

Standing on the sidewalk, backlit by the recently bright lamps of the parking lot, Dani and Hideo stared back at Badger. They smiled broadly at the store owner, but their countenances didn't have the same looks of happiness as they met his gaze. Instead, something like predatory expectation lay under their professional grins.

Badger's own smile wilted under their stares, and he suddenly didn't feel particularly joyful. Licking his lips, he tried to avoid holding eye contact for too long, and he then frowned, feeling off-balance and out of his element.

"Mr. Badger?" asked Dani, flashing her badge and continuing her shark-like grin. "If we could have a few minutes of your time, it would be appreciated."

#

Moments later, Dani stood in the middle of the now well-lit store. She held a thick folder in her hand, and she gazed down with an expansive grin at the brightly colored artistry on its front.   On the cover were the images of a wizard and warrior fighting a skeleton over a green background. The image was attractive in a cheaply drawn sort of way, like it had originally been drawn by a not-so-talented but eager teenage artist. Written in garish lettering across the image were the words *Tomb of Horrors.*

Standing to Dani's side, Hideo peered down at the inelegant folder. "What's that?"

Raising her eyebrows, Dani looked at her partner with a triumphant smirk. "Only one of the best gaming modules ever made. A true classic."

Exasperated, Hideo turned his gaze to Badger, who stood several feet away and had a similar look of resigned superiority, like he had long ago been privy to the knowledge of the secret of life.

Glancing between the two, Hideo appeared confused as to who was the bigger alien. "Wonderful. It's good to see that at least I managed to leave middle school at some point."

"Come on, Hideo," said Dani, batting her eyes. "Join us on the dark side. This stuff makes life worth living. Besides, gamers make better lovers."

Hideo grinned for a moment, then became mortified as he processed her words. With no quick response, a deep blush colored his cheeks.

Suddenly stopping her mock-seductive appearance, Dani dropped the module onto a shelf with the other forty-year-old gaming literature. Turning to Badger, the grin was gone from her face, and her interrogating focus made the store owner's own amusement melt away. In the blink of an eye, she was all business.

"So, Terry is a customer of yours?" asked Dani, clearly already knowing the answer.

Badger responded with a halting and boyish tone. "Uhh…yeah. He comes in…sometimes."

Dani continued with an icy stare and bitchy voice, two facets of femininity that every man since Adam met Eve had known at one time or another. "Sometimes? Like once a month, or once a day?"

"Usually…a couple times a week," Badger stammered, looking over to Hideo in a plea for help. Hideo shrugged, as if to say, *I'm not getting involved.*

Breathing deep and leaning back, Badger's voice became even less sure of himself. "Why are you asking about him? He's a good guy."

Ignoring Badger's question, Dani stepped closer to the awkward and unhygienic man. Overweight and six feet tall, Badger was at least twice her size, but he looked like a man in full retreat from a superior enemy.

"And what type of things did Mr. Brandt purchase in this den of geekdom," asked Dani, raising an eyebrow.

For a while, there was no answer, and the detectives assumed patient poses as they waited for a reply. Badger glanced repeatedly between them, not knowing how to talk or what to say.

"I'm not sure I want to answer that," said Badger. "This is a private business—."

Hideo interrupted Badger with a shake of his head and a chuckle. "I can feel you starting to get brave, Mr. Badger. Like you're going to become a hero to your subset of loserdom here. You should rethink that, like right away, because we're looking into some killings."

Badger's features grew worried, then overtly fearful. He gestured out the door, towards the world outside. "Killings? You think Terry is killing people?"

Hideo let the question go unanswered, letting his eyes bug out at the suggestion and looking over at Dani.

"So again, Mr. Badger, what things does he usually buy from you?" Dani asked.

Giving in, Badger motioned to the display case full of play figures. "He mostly buys figures for the games he runs. He just picked up an elven mage this morning."

"Runs?" asked Hideo.

"Yeah, he's a Dungeon Master, one of the best there is," replied Badger. "If someone wants a game at their home, he goes there, if they can afford it."

"So, Terry buys figures here," Dani said. "What else?"

Badger gestured back to the "Witchcraft" area of the store, which was more disorganized than the rest of the area and packed tightly with mix-and-match books and personal items. "He's got some stuff from that section in the past. Also, some regular character and monster books."

"What kind of 'stuff?'" asked Hideo, writing in his notepad.

Searching his memory, Badger thought through Terry's visits to the store. "Well, a lot of those things I buy used from whoever wants to sell. Things from the attic, estate sales…whatever. It's mostly fake magic books or semi-occult stuff. Some people like to play like they're gaming for real."

Nodding, Dani turned and paced several yards away, letting her eyes drift around the place. After a moment of consideration, she looked back to Badger. "So, Terry might be in this for real?"

Confused at the question, Badger ran his hand over his lightly stubbled chin. Taking his time, he drawled out his response, like each word was precise and thought out. "I think he's a good guy who likes to play games, like most of my customers. He's always been nice to me, and he…supports my store."

Chuckling, Dani didn't immediately reply. Instead, she wandered back a few aisles and looked down at a cluttered magazine rack. Reaching down, she pulled out a random copy of an old magazine with half-clothed witches dancing around a cauldron, like they were auditioning to be slutty enchantresses. Dani held the book up, and Hideo looked up from his writing long enough to smile at the image.

"I can see why a teenager would like to read this," said Dani, letting a mild grin play across her lips. "But I wonder, what does a thirty-nine-year-old man see in witchcraft and the occult? Who believes this stuff is real?"

Folding his book, Hideo tucked it into his suit pocket. "My guess is someone who has crazy ideas about reality. Someone who might not know or care about real-world suffering."

Tilting her head in agreement, Dani returned the magazine to the rack and walked back to Badger. Leaning close, her tone dropped, and she became kind, with a genuine smile and pleasant demeanor—like they were the best of comrades. "You mentioned he's one of the best Dungeon Masters? You must know of some people he likes to play with? Because…we'd really like to meet them, and…your input would be kept strictly confidential."

Badger thought for a while, gulping several times as he considered her question. Collecting himself, he became resolute and spoke softly. "He has a game he runs out in Lincoln on the weekends. Some rich guys who pay him really well. That's all I know…and I'm not sure I want to know anything else."

#

Outside of the gym was largely empty, with only a few residents taking late-night strolls along the wide sidewalk in front of the quiet health club. A few cars eased by on the streets that framed two sides of the workout facility, and traffic lights clicked as they changed colors in silent admission to the reduced traffic that attended the area at such a late hour on a weeknight. On the building's exterior, the glowing light of a timed bulb cast its periodic illumination from a colorful sign that read "Never Stop Fitness."

A small parking lot near the facility was empty at this time of night, except for an older green Suzuki Samurai parked across two spaces. Somewhere in the distance, the screams of a temper tantrum from a child were audible, seemingly carried across the nearly vacant streets by the warm summertime wind.

The immaculate windows running each side of the gym's entrance were unique in that they allowed people from both sides to easily see each other. In this way, little privacy was offered to people on either side of the glass, making a discreet workout impossible.

In truth, this was an intentional aspect of the building's design, because it catered to the ego of bodybuilders inside— as well as a substantial number of gawkers who often enjoyed ogling them from the public exterior. Muscle-bound people were always of interest to the outside world, so showcasing their strenuous workout regimen was certainly a logical decision on the gym owner's part.

Inside the gym, Alex strode from the locker room with a determined look on his face. Prepped for battle, he was a man who lived for this moment, a time when he felt like he could be himself as he sought chiseled human perfection from lifting weights.

Alex moved to the unmanned front counter of the business, where during normal business hours someone was always there to sell energy drinks, coffees, bottled water, or any of the varieties of special granola bars that went for a four hundred percent markup under the clear-glass display area. Reaching behind the counter, he increased the volume on the heavy metal music that belted from wall-mounted speakers throughout the place.

Alex, this man who had bowled over Terry when the dumpy gamer was leaving the convenience store, had long since forgotten about that brief encounter. He was the type of person whose mind only focused on heightening his musculature, and there was nothing he despised more than weakness and idle time. So, the memory of that scrawny and pathetic creature had quickly dissipated from his mind. His pursuit of bodybuilding glory meant focusing purely on improving his physique, something that took most of his time and thoughts.

In fact, there was rarely a day that passed when Alex's workout and consequent rigid eating habits took less than five hours of his time, such was his commitment to this lifestyle. He lived day-to-day by his self-styled motto of *take what is yours and leave the rest behind.*

Of course, the fact that he lived with his mom and spent much of his personal training income on supplements, plentiful eating of meat, and acquiring steroids did not cause him to doubt himself—those things were just the price of admission to being a monster. He wanted to be the best, which meant doing what it took to sculpt the perfect and enormous body, whatever the price.

Moving to a bench, Alex clanked several weights into place on the bar as he got ready to start his bench press. Locking the collars into place on the outside of the 45-pound weights, he settled in for his warm-up. He began pushing out repetitions to the beat of the inspiring music, feeling blood flow into his enormous pectoral muscles as he cranked out fifteen reps at two hundred and twenty-five pounds.

For Alex, the weight was low—his maximum press was more than five hundred pounds—but he liked to take it easy as he settled into his workout. He had friends in the business that short-circuited their whole livelihoods by attacking the initial weights and moving up too quickly—with the predictable result of injuring themselves in the process.

Alex saw getting hurt as laziness, because to be the best was not just a matter of weight, but instead not hurting yourself as you trained. Get huge and become as strong as humanly possible, but don't end up on a six-month furlough of convalescence in the process. Every time he saw a fellow gym rat go down with an injury due to lifting too high a weight, he scoffed at the individual and looked at their pain as a form of Darwinism, which weeded out the weak and stupid.

After stacking more weights on, Alex pressed through several more repetitions, grunting in the process and finishing with a grimace. Popping up, he faced himself in one of the mirrors and flexed. Bulging veins and slabs of muscle responded with impressive striation, and he nodded in self-important contentedness.

As he shot a double-bicep flex to evaluate the balance of his arm size, something bothered Alex from the mirror. A man stood outside the front window of the gym, and Alex could see the figure in the reflection, watching him and standing still. Spinning around, Alex focused outward, directly looking at the strange observer.

The man outside was dressed in a funny brown robe, the type that was often seen in representations of old church people who took vows of something or other. Alex knew less about church clothing from long ago than he did about modern geopolitical events, which was to say, not very much at all, and he tilted his head, confused at what the person might want.

Trying to ignore the dude, Alex laid down on the bench and finished another set of exercises, pressing the weight up until he could barely finish it. Breathing deep from his exertion, he sat up to revel in the moment for a job well completed. His brain, engorged in exercise endorphins that made him feel euphoric, made the world seem brighter and more vivid as he concentrated on his next specific workout task.

Looking up, Alex was surprised to see the robed stranger was now inside the building. He had not heard the man enter, which Alex knew set off a bell as the door opened. Shocked, Alex stared at this odd individual more closely.

The man had his hood pulled over his face, so that even in the well-lit room, his features were still hidden. Only a bit of the fellow's chin was visible under the hood, but what could be seen showed the skin was…strange, almost of a gray color. His frame was thin, and the bizarre robe hung off his slim body with room to spare. *Obviously, this ain't a weightlifter. Who the fuck?*

"What are you looking at?" demanded Alex, and he stood up, flexing his frame to intimidate the man, something that always worked to bully all the pipsqueaks he ran across in daily life. "You got a problem?"

Except, the man didn't respond like Alex thought he would. Instead, the stranger bladed himself off to Alex and got into an odd fighting stance. The result was this person, not even half his weight, acted like he wanted to fight.

Chuckling, Alex was surprised at the Chutzpah of this odd guy.

Though overtly cocky, something deep inside Alex's brain began to scream, trying to warn him of a situation that was off in some very disturbing way. But because Alex was a confident and not very wise man, he ignored the internal alarm bells.

As Alex stepped forward, he puffed out his chest like a human version of a peacock, ready to crush this insolent little dude. He didn't know how or why the man was here, but this pussy was going to be sorry for fucking with him.

With a movement that was almost too fast to see, the figure lunged forward and push-kicked Alex in the upper chest with a THUD, sending him backward and flipping over an unoccupied bench. Landing with a clank and sprawled amongst several dumbbells, the muscled man stared up, eyes wide and uncomprehending.

Not quite understanding how he got there, Alex rubbed his chest and grimaced from the riveting pain that came from the spot where he was struck. Taking his time, he struggled up, trying to come to grips with the situation. "You…piece of shit. Who the fuck are you…why…?"

Coming to his full height, Alex focused in on the stranger, and now the lunatic had Alex's undivided attention. Reaching over, Alex grabbed a long and heavy 45-pound barbell from atop a squat rack. Hefting it with ease, he gripped it in a baseball stance and moved carefully toward the waiting stranger.

Screaming his own version of a battle cry, Alex swung the bar in a wide arc as he rushed forward. The robed man deftly dodged two of the swings, stepping back to create some distance between the sudden combatants.

When the stranger got too close to a wall to step any farther, he moved into an incoming swing, and a loud crack from the bar striking his arm made the stranger's arm go completely limp. Jumping to the side, the man backed up some more, letting his broken arm hang loosely as he waited for Alex's next move.

Grinning, Alex knew he had this crazy fuck now. This guy had attacked him first, and judging from the pain in his chest, had really hurt him. There wasn't a court in the state that was gonna hold it against him to beat the guy to death—hopefully, anyway. For the first time in his life, Alex was going to get to kill someone, and that thought just made his smile grow wider. *The fucker has it coming.*

As Alex reared back to brain his opponent, his adversary struck out with a brutal roundhouse kick. Striking Alex in the upper thigh, his femur SNAPPED with a sickening sound, and he crumpled to the ground, his maimed leg bending oddly to the side.

Flailing on the gym floor, Alex tried to throw the barbell at the guy, but another swift kick from the stranger intercepted the clumsy missile and batted it aside. Stepping closer to the injured weightlifter, the bizarre man wasn't in a hurry as he closed the distance.

Screaming in agony and fear, Alex tried to pull himself away from his aggressor. Shrieking as he clawed at the ground, with wide eyes looking somewhere—anywhere—for help, he crawled toward his workout bench, the place where he had just been enjoying his workout. Only a few moments ago and the world had seemed so right.

As he got close to the bench, Alex awkwardly pulled himself around to face his unknown foe. Looking up at the man, he was dumbfounded and terrified, with eyes that prayed for relief from the incoming nightmare.

The stranger stopped for a moment, and his head tilted, as if he was considering what to do next. With a smooth motion, the attacker pulled back his hood, revealing his unseen face to the cowering bodybuilder below.

Seeing something he could not understand, Alex began screaming and wailing unintelligibly. His shrieks and garbled pleas for leniency merged into a despairing mishmash of fearful gibberish as the assailant walked slowly toward him. As he got closer, the squeals of the huge man, sprawled on the floor and awaiting his fate, grew louder and more girlish.

The bravado of Alex's entire life up to this point was gone, lost in the reality of the brutal moment, and only a scared man who wanted to live another day remained. His pleading eyes stared up at the incoming attacker, and in that moment, Alex sought mercy from this bizarre attacker, the type that he had never shown himself in a lifetime of bullying and ridicule of others.

From outside the gym, the night and streets were unoccupied and quiet. Alex's screams and the sound of the loud rock song could be easily heard, if only someone was there to listen to them. Shortly, the screams were cut short by several cracking sounds, like that of wood being split from inside.

Then, only the faint sound of the workout music continued.

Chapter Twelve

The office was relatively small, and because it had two large desks facing each other, not much space remained to move around inside the room. Making the area more cluttered, two filing cabinets stood against either end of the oblong room, and a long marking board filled with barely legible scribblings leaned against a small couch to the side.

A couple of the walls were covered with framed photos of far-off places, with ancient Roman ruins and the Great Wall of China being the most noticeable locations. On another wall, there was only one large print, that of the famous UFO photo on the *X-Files*, but instead of the writing on the original stating, "I want to believe," there was added in a black marker the sarcastic words, "I want to believe in this crappy fake photo."

Dani sat at one side of the strange arrangement, twirling a pen in her dexterous fingers, while on the other, Hideo was reclined with his head braced by his clasped hands. She had a look of deep thought on her features, but her partner had the dreamy stare of someone who was soon to take a nap.

Exasperated, Dani cleared her throat. "And then there were three."

"Huh?" asked Hideo, coming awake.

"Murders," replied Dani. "In a town that usually has less than that in one year. At this rate, our humble city of Elk Grove will join the ranks of Sacramento and Hoboken as places you'd never want to live."

Confused, Hideo scrunched up his face. "Why Hoboken? I mean, if you're gonna come up with places that are scary and crime-ridden, you got Phili, or Detroit, maybe Memphis…why choose that place? I'm not even sure it's still inhabited. Is it?"

Thinking about it for a moment, Dani nodded her reluctant agreement. "I don't know, it just seems like such a mafia-ee place. Ho…bo…ken, makes me think of Sicilian gangsters— men with scarred faces and pasta stains on their expensive shirts."

"You're weird, Dani, and this is coming from a guy that's been told the same his whole life."

Dani nodded again, agreeing with Hideo's evaluation of her character. "Anyway, having killings pop up daily is not going to make tourism increase in our whereabouts. We should notify the Chamber of Commerce to change our branding. We could become 'dead-elksville,' or maybe 'murder grove.'"

"These are trying times we live in," replied Hideo, not looking too concerned and chuckling. Leaning forward in his chair, he fumbled around in a paper bag and took out a Tupperware container.

Keeping her thoughtful look, Dani stood and walked to the printer, where she took two printed photos from the tray. Moving back to her seat, she dropped them in front of Hideo. "From the CCTV at the gym."

The first photo showed the hooded figure in the lobby with his face covered. The next showed the back of the killer's shaved head. Facing away, the bald man's arm hung limp, clearly injured as he looked off-screen. Surprisingly, the images were clear.

"And, of course, we can't see his face," said Dani.

Setting down the prints, Hideo was disturbed. There was something about the killer that seemed off, like he didn't belong there. Sort of like if they had a real-life and very distinct photo of an ancient medieval festival—the murderer seemed out of place with the technology. "Dude looks creepy."

"He looks like a monk."

Bemused, Hideo raised his tone. "You mean like the Dalai Lama?"

"No," replied Dani, rolling her eyes. "More like a warrior monk. They are their own class in RPGs. At least, they were when I was a kid."

"RPGs?" asked Hideo, growing more perplexed.

"Role-Playing Games, like our favorite security guard likes to play."

Exasperated, Hideo leaned forward and stared at Dani through the slit between his dual monitors. "Did you take classes on how to be strange?"

Not answering him, Dani leaned back and dropped into deep thought.

Returning to his bag, Hideo extracted another container and opened it. A foul odor wafted through the room, and Dani wrinkled her nose in disgust.

"What?" asked Hideo, growing defensive. "It's Kimchi. Fermented cabbage. The Koreans gobble the stuff up. Sixty million people can't be wrong."

"I'm sure it's…lovely," Dani said, leaning in front of her screen and beginning to type. "So, now we have a dead fitness freak. Beaten to death by a monk. That's not something you hear every day."

"Beaten to death? Like, with his hands?"

"With his feet, too," responded Dani, continuing to type. "That's what the report says. No other weapons of any kind were used to kill a man that weighed two-hundred and sixty-five pounds. It's like Peewee Herman pummeling The Rock to death."

Hideo leaned down and took several bites from his meal, slurping contentedly on the noxious contents. After annoying Dani with the sound for a while, he responded with an impressed expression, raising his eyebrows at the thought of such an amazing feat. "Haven't ever heard of something like that. Makes me want to take up martial arts…or buy more guns."

Dani chuckled and continued clacking, her fingers darting across the keyboard.

"But I don't see any connection to Brandt," said Hideo, holding up his chopsticks and practicing closing them on empty air, like he was Mr. Miyagi trying to catch flies in *The Karate Kid*. "He doesn't look like he's been in a gym…ever."

Finishing her work, Dani stood and looked down at Hideo. She had a gleam in her eye that he knew well, like she found something only she could've figured out. She spoke in a low tone, as if she was soon to reveal some great and monumental truth. "No obvious connection, no. But I have an idea."

"Pray tell."

"Somehow, Brandt has himself a little following," Dani said, and she walked over to the UFO photo frame, looking at it with a frown. "He's become the Charles Manson of the gaming world."

"Like a geek messiah?"

Ignoring Hideo's grin and comical retort, Dani continued. "And, he's using his nerd acolytes to settle scores with people he hates. Sort of like he's become an avenger for wrongs committed against him—perceived or otherwise. Sounds like a movie…or should be."

Thinking for a moment, Hideo nodded noncommittally. "Could be…kinda makes sense. But who are these followers of his that are willing to murder at will? Never heard of commitment like that. And how are these gaming cultists getting away? Nutcases like this should be easy to find in a land where sweatpants and jeans are the most common forms of dress."

There was silence for some time as both pondered Dani's suggestion. Hideo continued his doubtful stare while Dani worked something through in her mind.

Coming to a decision, Dani moved back to her desk, where she rotated her monitor for Hideo to see the contents. On the screen was the profile of "Jerome Sanders," with his handsome photo and biographical information in neat columns underneath. At the bottom, under "occupation," was the profession "lawyer."

"I'm not sure of the logistics of this," Dani said, trying to imagine how a rich lawyer could be pulling overtime as a loyal henchman killer. "The whole thing is like a batshit-crazy soup, and we've gotta find the ingredients that made it. I think we can start with Brandt's game in Lincoln, and we better get some answers before anyone else pisses him off."

Chapter Thirteen

The mall wasn't busy at this time of day, with only a few shoppers shuffling between several clothing stores and small eateries at this midpoint of the summer day. In the interior, far to the inside of the double-decker mall plaza, a host of dinging cars plied their way around a small track in a kids-centered race display. The thuds of colliding vehicles mixed with shouts of joy from youngsters taking part in a birthday party bumper-car race, making for a pleasant scene in the air-conditioned interior of the vast shopping area.

At the entry point of the mall, just inside a brace of large glass entry doors, stood a large and artfully constructed fountain. Water tumbled from atop a series of successive boulders, cascading into a raucous and glittering pool in the common area, where a host of people sitting on nearby benches were taking a moment to rest from the outside heat.

To the side of the bubbling fountain was a small flower shop. A bored teen stood behind a small counter, and to her side and back was a barrage of vases, overflowing with all manner of different-colored flowers and green plants. With a thick wad of gum in her mouth, the disinterested girl gave the appearance of an unenthusiastic tour guide standing in front of a well-tended jungle.

Terry walked through the automatic doors of the front entrance. Peering around, he spied the small flower shop and jaunted happily toward it, all the while displaying a look that told the world all was well in his humble life. As he moved past clusters of strangers, he made eye contact and exchanged contented nods with everyone he could, trying to be the nice guy he always imagined himself to be. For once in a very long time, he felt like he was part of the ebb and flow of societal interaction, and it was a feeling he immensely enjoyed.

Stepping in front of the teenager, Terry was surprised that she barely paid attention to him. In fact, it appeared she was going out of her way to ignore him. Glancing at Terry, she seemed to think she would catch a horrible infection if she so much as offered him a smile of greeting.

Taking stock of Terry with his plastered-down hair, clean-shaven but nicked face, and a dark sweater looking like it had last been stylish in the 1950s, the cashier couldn't imagine him having a reason to buy flowers. In a society where people often didn't know how to be mean and rude, and indeed went out of their way to lie in order to protect feelings, this young woman had no problem doing so, which at least was an honest approach. She wouldn't win any customer awards for her attitude, and it was obvious that for her, that was perfectly fine.

Terry didn't let the rudeness bother him, such was his state of optimism and outward joy. He grinned and pointed to an exquisite arrangement that included several roses and intertwined garnishes of attractive leaves.

"Is that your most expensive set of flowers?" asked Terry. "I want only the best."

Blinking at Terry, the young lady's voice was doubtful. "What do you want them for?"

"For my…girlfriend," said Terry, and he pronounced the word with a sense of reverence, like he was speaking of the Virgin Mary.

There was silence for a moment, and the cashier didn't try to hide her doubt about Terry's love prospects. She had heard in her life's limited experience that there was "someone for everyone," but staring at this chubby and disgusting man, with his reddish face and just-visible blackheads on his too-large nose, she couldn't believe anyone in the history of the world would ever be so desperate.

Breathing deep, the arrogant twit finally offered an insincere smile. "I think a nice bouquet of roses would work. Should I put them in a vase…or just wrap 'em in a plastic sleeve?"

"A vase would be great, thanks," replied Terry. "Please, make it so."

The teen nodded and reached for the flowers. As she began snipping away pieces of the stems to make them more presentable, Terry's grin grew wider. *She's gonna love it. I've gotta be the luckiest guy in the world.*

While Terry beamed with pride and adoring expectation for the night ahead, he didn't notice the cashier rolling her eyes and shaking her head.

#

The apartment was cozy, with a thick-cushioned couch and loveseat arranged over plush carpet and facing an enormous flat-screen TV. A clean kitchen with dark Formica countertops was attached to the living room, and a small kitchen table stood on the linoleum floor that subdivided the spaces.

To the back of the living room, a small hallway exited toward a large bedroom and bathroom. An assortment of pictures, both of photo and artistic prints, covered most of the available space on the walls of the room and hallway, with the themes of butterflies, birds, and gorgeous sunsets representing the most popular subjects for decoration.

Emma stood in the kitchen, looking down at several sizzling pans and boiling bots. Moving fastidiously, she monitored the montage of cooking food, making sure the sauce, noodles and sizzling meat were at the right temperature to ensure a pleasant outcome. Leaning down, she sipped pasta sauce from a steaming ladle to test its culinary reliability.

Even though she was cooking, Emma was showered and dressed well in a simple summer dress, like she had arranged herself to be ready for something more than just a fine meal. Stepping away from the various concoctions, she glanced at a wall-mounted clock with an image of Patrick Swayze under the clock's hands. The time was two minutes before 6:00 PM.

As if in answer to Emma's expectant gaze, a firm knock came from the front door. The muted rap was barely audible, as the steel core of the substantial door made sound difficult to hear. Breaking into a happy grin, Emma wiped her hands on a wet towel and moved to disengage several locks running the length of the door frame.

After unlocking the door, she pulled it open, her eyes going wide in anticipation. A huge bouquet of roses greeted her, behind which was the smiling face of Terry. Looking at Emma, who was made up and waiting to serve him dinner, Terry was elated at his good fortune.

"Happy International Women's Day," said Terry, pressing the flowers through the door a little too abruptly.

Flinching to avoid being struck by the flowers, Emma blinked and reassumed her pleasant smile. Motioning Terry inside, she moved to the kitchen and set the vase on the counter.

"International Woman's Day?" asked Emma.

"Yeah, it's a big deal in the rest of the world," responded Terry. "I thought you would like to know you're appreciated."

Emma's smile faltered, and she picked up her phone to do a quick search on Woman's Day. Pursing her lips, she lowered the phone to the kitchen counter and sounded less enthusiastic. "Isn't that day in March?"

"Yeah, I guess so. I just thought I should bring something special for our third date," Terry said, keeping his upbeat expression. He wasn't going to let anything ruin their special night together, and that meant he had to focus on being confident.

Nodding, Emma moved to the simmering dinner on the stove. As she picked at the meat with a spatula, a cloud descended over her features. She had recently spoken with her mom about this issue with guys, where Emma had lamented that the men available either wanted a porn star for a girlfriend, or they were so socially inept that life by herself seemed like a better alternative.

For her part, Emma knew that being a cashier at a convenience store meant her marketability wasn't the highest. She also knew she wasn't gorgeous and could best be defined as plain. This meant that she had to accept that her potential mates wouldn't exactly be doctors or look like Chris Pratt, and she saw herself as a realist in this regard. Unfortunately, the few times she'd met guys in the last year, the results weren't stellar, and sooner or later, she wasn't able to look past their character flaws.

A night she had been looking forward to seemed to deflate into the realization she may have just struck loser pay dirt again, and she frowned in disappointment. Sniffing the aromatic food, she looked back at Terry, realizing that this guy had better get more normal by the end of the night. As it now stood, if she took Terry to see her mother, her mom would have a heart attack from the nerdy vibe he was throwing off. *International Woman's Day? In late August?*

Worse, Terry was acting like they were already a thing, which usually led to possessiveness and inflated expectations within a couple of months. It was one thing to be needy when you'd been together a few years, but on the third date, it was a flashing red sign to run for the hills. When she first became single, she had met a possessive psycho like that, and that was what led to the reinforced front door she had installed with the help of a contractor friend.

From the living room, Terry was unaware of anything being wrong. Flashing a grin, he dropped into the couch and pulled a bowl of tortilla chips close. As he began munching away, he grabbed her remote and turned on the television, like he had just found a new home.

Chapter Fourteen

Jerome Sanders had an intense expression on his face, the focused look of a committed and obsessed man. Sitting grimly at his desk, he stared ahead, concentrating as if his very survival depended on it. On his head, he had large, brightly colored headphones, causing him to appear like a determined fighter pilot in the limited light of the room.

Alone in his dim office, light streamed through the window behind Sanders, and the tall trees outside his window waved gently in the midday breeze. Directly in front of him was an enormous computer monitor, set at just the right angle for him to have a perfect viewing experience.

Made with the latest and best TV technology, the screen's image was a bright and an absolutely enthralling experience, with a vast subterranean habitat of scary and endless caverns lying before him. His vision in that computer world was hued in red, stalactites hung everywhere from the ceiling, and the incessant drip of distant liquids amongst the raw cave structures made the scene odd and primordial.

Abruptly, a demonic creature lunged from the darkness, a horrific and misshapen being with a mouth of razor teeth and a face of black scales and red eyes. Sanders began blasting the horrid thing with his shotgun, and he leaned to the side like he was dodging it in real life. Several more beasts rushed from the surrounding layers of rock and shadows, and he expertly destroyed them with further booms from his fierce weapon.

Threatening and wicked howls from the rest of the cavern reached his ears with perfect resonance through his expensive wireless headphones, and Sanders knew he was in for the fight of his life. They were coming for him, these hordes of devilish entities. With his pulse pounding and a sense of dread filling his panicked features, he knew that any moment could be his last. His eyes darted around the screen, looking for the next wicked enemy to emerge from the hellish background.

Suddenly, several long buzzing sounds interrupted the blood-curdling battle, and Sanders was taken away from his moment of frenzied survival in the underworld.

Dropping his headphones to the side, Sanders frowned as he pressed a button on the phone console to his left. "Shit, Chloe, I told you I'm busy and would be the rest of the afternoon. What is it?"

After a hesitant pause, a chagrined female voice responded through the speaker. "I'm sorry, Mr. Sanders…I have two detectives here to see you. They said it's very important."

Looking back at his screen, Sanders saw bolded blood-red writing announce, "You are Dead." He scowled in response, and irritation filled his chest with throbbing annoyance, making him want to punch the monitor. It was bad enough to have a job where he argued with pricks most of the day, but now he had cops visiting? He was used to conflict, but he didn't practice criminal law, so a visit by law enforcement was a new wrinkle in his rather humdrum legal existence.

Still, Sanders realized this could be interesting, and it might break up his day more than his latest fight in the demon lands. Sounding a bit less obnoxious, he responded. "OK, send them in. Thank you."

Moments later, there was a tap on the door. After Sanders bid them to enter, Dani stuck her head in, gently making her way into the office with her hands in her pockets. As she moved into the room, Hideo came in behind her, and each looked at their host's stern face, affecting fake smiles as they measured the worth of the seated attorney.

Though there were two leather chairs present, Sanders didn't offer them a seat. Instead, he remained quiet, keeping his face a mask of seriousness. Reclining in his chair, he let silence keep the detectives occupied.

After a moment, Sanders broke the quiet, speaking in an aloof and arrogant tone. "What can I do for you?"

Dani let her gaze wander the room, taking in rows of law books, a print of the Constitution, and a beautiful bust of the Roman Emperor Tiberius Claudius on a table against the wall. Dani had a class in Roman history in college, and she was able to recognize the leader's face as one of the first ancient emperors who had codified the legal profession into their society. The fact that Sanders also knew this historical fact meant she was dealing with a man who was refined, or at least thought of himself that way, meaning he wasn't stupid and did his homework. Realizing this meant she also needed to show a backbone in interacting with him, as she had long ago learned weakness invites ridicule from such people—never cooperation.

Interestingly, an immense drawing of a vividly colored Red Dragon also took up space on the wall. The enormous and exquisitely drawn creature was perched on the top of a small grass-covered hill, with its eyes and fierce gaze focused on an armed and armored knight below it, ready to do battle. The scene was beautiful and engaging, especially for those that liked such imagery.

The dragon image took up most of the wall near a fold-out treadmill, which indicated a sense of reverence from Sanders, and showed Sanders' inclination for gaming was not merely a passing fancy but was probably something that offered great joy for the experienced attorney.

Dani spoke in a respectful tone as her eyes turned to Sanders. "We have come to talk to you about Terry Brandt. Do you know him?"

Sanders' face didn't flinch. "Should I? You're here in my office—for God knows what. You tell me."

Hideo, who stood near the corner looking at the dragon image, spoke up. His voice was less respectful. "Mr. Sanders, it has come to our attention that you know Mr. Brandt. It's not a secret, so maybe we can avoid the verbal jousting we both know you're capable of. We thought it prudent to approach—"

"Your prudence isn't my concern, detective," replied Sanders, cutting him off. "Tell me what you want, clearly. I'm a busy man."

Taking a step closer to his desk, Dani continued her polite tone. "We want to know everything about him. He's a suspect in some very serious crimes, crimes that directly relate to the games at your home on the weekend."

Chuckling, Sanders leaned back farther in his chair. He didn't appear surprised she knew of the games—and obviously wasn't worried about it. Squeaking as he rocked forward and back, he connected his fingers in a prayer-like pose and stared at Dani. "If I know this man, and by no means am I saying I do, what business is it of yours? Do you think I would rat to the government on any of my friends or associates? Tell me you are not that stupid."

Dani grinned at the insult, nodding with a pleasant expression. "Fair enough. Let me put it this way: we think Terry is having people killed, and we think he's using people he plays games with to make it happen."

Taking a deep breath, Dani stepped to the side and dropped into one of the chairs. Taking a moment to get comfortable, she kept the same measured tone. "I can also see that you're a pompous asshole who would be happy to frustrate us in any way you can. It's in your DNA—assholes can't help themselves."

Sanders raised an eyebrow at her candor, smirking and obviously enjoying the insult, but he remained quiet as he waited for more.

"It's obvious to me that you're not involved," said Dani, gesturing to the comfortable and attractive room, as well as the pleasant garden area that lay beyond his office window. "Anybody as smart and secured in their life as you isn't going to get involved with a loser who murders people. That would be irrational and illogical, and lawyers—even assholes—are usually the opposite of those things."

Several moments passed, and to Sanders' credit, the reveal of her suspicions didn't cause even a hint of surprise on his features. As his squeaking chair continued its grating sound, he moved his gaze between the detectives and considered his response.

"I've known Terry for three years," Sanders said, finally adopting the monotoned and dispassionate voice of a guarded opponent. "And…he has always been an excellent shepherd of our games during that time."

Hideo wrote in his notebook, looking up periodically and fixing Sanders with his own dispassionate look. Not one to miss a word, he locked on the attorney as his pen darted across the small paper. As Dani once told him, it was good he could read his own notes because nobody else had a hope of transcribing his gobbledygook.

Standing, Sanders spoke clearly, annunciating each syllable in a manner that implied both detectives were idiots. "He has also never been anything but accommodating and nice. If you think he's capable of killing people, then you are even more clueless than I imagine most cops to be. You need to look elsewhere."

Walking to the door, Sanders opened it and motioned out toward the lobby. "If you want to know more than that, then 'I'll see you in court,' as they say. Have a good afternoon."

After a shrug at one another, Dani and Hideo moved to exit the room. On the way out, Sanders made sure to engage each of them with an insincere and mirthful smile.

When the door clicked shut, Sanders' expression grew instantly serious, and he returned to his desk. Reversing his chair, he stared out the window and took in the well-trimmed grass and hedges, in addition to a variety of colored flowers and bushes ringing an area where people could sit on benches and enjoy a break or extended lunch. After a long while, he came to a decision and spun around. Thinking carefully, he hesitantly grabbed his office phone.

Dialing a long series of numbers, he was greeted at the other end by an inaudible answer.

"John?" asked Sanders, letting his voice fill with an incredulous tone. "Yeah, I'm doing well, thanks. Listen, no way in hell you're gonna believe what just happened…"

#

The kitchen was full of activity in the late evening. From several pans on the stove came the sound of sizzling sausage and popping bacon, as well as the fizz of bubbling scrambled eggs over the gentle heat of a gas-lit flame. The sound of twanging country music played from an old radio at the end of the countertop, providing a mild, if depressing, mood for the room.

Toast popped up from a toaster with a THUNK, and Terry hurried suddenly into the kitchen from the back hallway. Dressed in a comfortable collared shirt, dark pants, and looking like he had recently showered, he was surprisingly presentable and clean for this time of day.

Removing the toast and setting it on a plate, he turned to the stove and began stirring the eggs. Looking to the side, he grabbed another of the skillets and scraped the meats onto the same plate, taking care to avoid spilling any of it as he hurried his meal preparation.

Moving throughout the rest of the kitchen, Terry tried to control the chaos of the moment. Grabbing a pair of glasses from a cabinet, he filled them with orange juice and moved to the kitchen table. Arranging a set place for the meal, he looked up just in time to see his father exit from the back of the apartment.

Open-mouthed, Wayne stared at the lively scene before him. "What the hell is going on? It's almost seven."

Sounding cheery, Terry pulled back a chair at the table and motioned toward it. "I know, Dad, I'm making breakfast."

"Huh?"

"You slept all day," Terry said. "So I thought you might be up for some breakfast."

Moving back to the stove, Terry picked up the steaming plate of food and added eggs to the pile of mismatched meats. Coming back to the table, he set it where he expected his father to sit.

Not quite knowing how to respond, Wayne walked over to the table and sat. Dumbfounded, he looked at Terry with open and disbelieving eyes, saying nothing as he tried to understand what was going on.

"You want pancakes, Dad?" Terry asked, reaching into a cabinet for a bag of ready-made mix. "I can make some in a couple of minutes."

Looking at his plate, Wayne evaluated the cooking. The eggs were browned, the meat was scorched, and the toast was without butter, but it at least looked edible. Grabbing a slice of bacon, he munched on the overly crisp end of it.

Chewing for a moment, Wayne's typically foul mood caught up with him. "Nah, I don't need no pancakes."

Returning from the kitchen with his own plate of food, Terry sat opposite his father. As he focused on Wayne, he went silent and appeared expectant, as if hoping for some conversation.

None was forthcoming. Scowling at the less-than-perfect food, Wayne stood and moved to the refrigerator, where he withdrew a bottle of vodka from the cabinet above the fridge. Coming back to his seat, he topped the orange juice with a generous helping of the liquor.

Now it was Wayne's turn to smile. Raising the glass, he gulped several mouthfuls of the liquid, and a hearty and contented grin crossed his features. Grabbing a sausage, he crammed the whole link into his mouth and followed it with another swig of his mixed drink.

Taking the silence as a time to talk, Terry spoke slowly, as if testing the waters for communication with his old man, something that hadn't happened in a long time. "Dad? I wanted to tell you about a girl I met. She's great…and I think she might be the one for me."

Setting down his glass, Wayne looked surprised and skeptical. "Girl? You aren't bothering those strippers again, are ya? Son, those women will never make a good lady for ya."

"She's not like that," responded Terry, shaking his head and blushing. "She's really beautiful…and is looking for a guy. I think I'm the perfect fit for her."

"Son, I've told ya before, you gotta take it slow with the ladies. Otherwise, ya just end up getting used."

Terry looked down, picking at his meat and considering Wayne's words. "No, not this one. We've already had three dates, and I'm gonna ask her to a movie tomorrow."

Shaking his head, Wayne poured more booze into his glass. "Well, have fun, anyway. At least get laid. Sometimes ya leave that porn on your computer, and they can hear it all the way next door. At least turn your sound down."

Blushing deep from Wayne's surprising knowledge of his self-administered romantic life, Terry could nevertheless see his dad wouldn't understand about Emma, at least not yet. Terry knew in his heart this could be true love—he would just have to show Wayne over time the true nature of Emma. Words would never be enough for him to describe her special place in his heart.

Holding up a finger, Terry realized he had forgotten something. Hurrying from the table, he went in the back to his bedroom as his dad stared weirdly after him. Returning, he set a large cardboard box near his father and indicated it with a happy nod of his head.

"What's that?" asked Wayne, tilting his head in confusion.

Terry didn't respond, and after a moment, Wayne sat his drink down and pulled the box closer to himself. Opening the lid, he slowly pulled a beautiful kitten from inside. The little cat was orange and white, and his pathetic little eyes looked up to Wayne as he mewled an almost-silent greeting.

Staring back at Terry, Wayne was in shock. A look of awed appreciation, something that he didn't know he could express to his son, crossed his face. Looking back to the kitten, Wayne's eyes teared up.

"You said you wanted to bring that stray cat from work," said Terry, keeping a warm smile. "On your last day of work…so I thought I could get you this little guy. He's not a black-and-white one, but he's had all his shots. The pound gives 'em out for free when they got too many."

Brooding in silence, Wayne didn't know what to say. His gaze moved several times between the kitten and his son, and a look of mourning filled his eyes, a look that portended memories of a young boy that had evolved into a cynical adult and an alcoholic long ago.

Something of that young man, so lost and forgotten, was still there in Wayne's sad expression. For just a moment, Wayne was subdued and childlike, lost in the vague recollections of a kid who would have died for such a present as this little kitty.

If something like this had been given to him as an abandoned boy, a child who had been taken away from his drug-addicted parents, he might have had hope when there was nothing else for him to live for.

"He could be a good friend to you," said Terry, interrupting Wayne's thoughts and trying to stay optimistic.

Wayne looked at the gorgeous eyes of the kitten for a few moments longer, lost in the need for protection he saw in those innocent orbs. Gulping, he considered hugging his son, knowing it was the nicest present he had ever received in his tortured and miserable life.

Standing, Wayne set the cat back into the box. Moving to the kitchen, he stared at the stove and avoided the gaze of his son. Inhaling deeply, he wiped tears away with the back of his hand.

"I don't need no damn cat," Wayne said, struggling through a wave of sadness. "I'll just have to feed it and clean up its crap. What man's got time for that?"

Lowering his eyes, Terry was sad. "I...just thought it would be nice to have around."

"Well, you thought wrong," exclaimed Wayne. "Again. You gotta learn to live in the real world. Nobody gives a shit about ya out there. YOU gotta take care of yourself—and fuck everyone else."

Hurriedly, Wayne grabbed a set of car keys from a holder on the refrigerator. Moving toward the door, he still avoided his son's eyes as he eased it open. "I'll be home late. Don't wait up for me."

With that, Wayne slammed the door shut and was gone.

Staring at the uneaten food, Terry's own eyes grew watery. For a long time, he sat there, with only the distant words of a sad song from George Jones to keep him company.

Picking himself up, Terry grabbed the cat's box and walked carefully with it to his room, leaving the mess of abandoned food to be thrown out later.

Chapter Fifteen

The day was overcast, and a brisk wind blew across a collection of green and orderly lawns. In patches across the turf were collections of dandelions, and the plants shed their parachute seeds in waves at each sudden rush of air in the morning's clear light.

In the background stood the three buildings of Benelux Capital's office complex, where sunrays from the cloudless day illuminated their windows in a squint-inducing shine. Surrounding the main structure were crowds of employees taking a break and getting a breath of fresh air in the unseasonably chilly weather.

Dani stood next to the barbecue area of the smaller building used for training by the Benelux Corporation. Pulling her coat tight, she grimaced at the cool weather and searched the surrounding area with confused eyes.

"It doesn't make any sense," said Dani, continuing to scour the tree line for something. "Moving that distance and not using the path…"

"No, it doesn't," replied Hideo, squatting and looking down at the spot where Darby had met his end. The ground there had long since been cleaned of any clues that might have been left from the murder, but Hideo still glared inquisitively at the spot where the rich executive had received his death blow.

Pointing to a distant spot to the northwest, Hideo chewed on something while shaking his head. "The security guard said our mystery killer was way over there, but he somehow ambushes the mogul here. No way to get that far without following Darby on his run."

"Which means there has to be two of them, right? That, or we have a seven-foot killer with a huge axe that runs like Usain Bolt—or faster."

Hideo stood and popped a handful of something into his mouth. Looking at Dani, he squinted with worry, knowing they were missing something important to the story. "The frames we have on him on the video show he's a monster. How many people in California are that big? Who wouldn't notice this guy? When I was a kid, I saw Hulk Hogan at a charity event, and I remember it like it was yesterday. Huge people trigger your mind to remember things."

Dani walked over to the ruined barbecue, running a finger over the curled metal edges at the point where the killer's sharp weapon slashed through most of the solid cooker. "Almost nobody would forget him, and even less would forget an axe-wielding, homicidal one. What are you eating?

Suddenly looking defensive, Hideo frowned. "Barbecued corn nuts. Is there anything I eat that meets your approval?"

"Apparently not. Chewing on flavored rocks is a real joy."

Grinning, Hideo exaggerated his chewing motion. Disgusted, Dani looked away.

"So, how does our giant or giants get out of here after whacking Mr. Wealthy Guy?" asked Dani, reassuming her professional tone. "He would be seen wherever he goes; every foot of the perimeter is recorded and archived."

"And, how did he get in here?" added Hideo. "Maybe he flew in on an ultralight?"

Chuckling, Dani nodded at the idea. "Can you imagine a four-hundred-pound giant, careening through the sky on one of those things?"

Smiling, Hideo shook his head. "Not even in one of your games."

There was silence for a time as both partners continued their visual check of the surrounding area, as if some explanation might present itself in the early light of day.

Breaking the quiet, Dani spoke in a considered tone. "Makes me think of an old friend."

"The giant or the ultralight?"

Slipping into her memories, Dani's smile waned. "Both, at least indirectly. When I was in college in New Mexico, I knew a guy, Everson Montgomery. He was easily the most boring and rational person you'd ever met."

"This should be good."

"Yeah, so Everson meets us for pizza one night, and he's as white as a ghost. He had that look people get when they come inches from death, like that dude whose car got hit by a train last year when he was stalled on the tracks. He was just able to jump out of the way before becoming railroad pizza."

Hideo nodded, still chewing.

"Anyway, so Everson just drove his girlfriend home in a remote area outside Albuquerque," Dani said. "They were driving along at night, and he said he saw this guy lurch in front of his car from out of nowhere."

Hideo raised his eyebrows in mock surprise. "Sounds amazing."

Ignoring the sarcasm, Dani continued. "He said the guy was dressed in really old clothes, like he was an old prospector, and he didn't notice the car or lights. He said the way the guy walked—or stumbled—was the creepiest thing he had seen in his life. Like he was from another time or place. Like he was out of sync with the moment, if that makes sense."

"It doesn't. If I remember right, Albuquerque is also full of weirdos."

"No doubt," said Dani. "But they stop within a couple seconds and get out to help prospector guy, thinking he's lost or starving or…something. When they look out over the field, there's nothing there. He's gone."

Doubtful, Hideo cocked his head. "It was nighttime. Darkness makes it kinda hard to see."

"That's what I thought, but that area has no trees. And most nights, you can see for miles under the moonlight. It interested me so much that I drove out to see the exact spot he stopped."

Hideo offered her a disbelieving grin, not trying to hide his skepticism.

"And when I saw where it happened, I knew something crazy had happened," Dani said, continuing in her best storyteller voice. "A cheetah running at a full clip would have been visible for a half-minute from the time they got out of the car."

Continuing his dubious gaze, Hideo rolled his yes. "So, you're saying a ghost killed Darby? That'll make for an interesting report—and a short career."

"I'm saying that sometimes there's no rational answer for things that happen. And, I'm starting to get that same feeling I had back then, when I looked over that clear field at night, like I was never gonna know the right answer to what Everson saw."

"Okay, then what should we do? Drive to New Mexico and ask the Night Gods who killed Darby?"

"We need to quit messing around," replied Dani, becoming more serious. "And pressure Brandt. I don't know how he's doing it, but he's our guy. Truth is, there might be something here we can't understand."

The reality of their current position was that they were at a loss to explain anything. Three murders had been committed without the slightest indication of who had done the deeds. Dani had overseen several investigations in her productive detective life, and it usually took about ten minutes to figure out how and why the acts had been committed.

Dani had always remarked to her coworkers that criminals were not only stupid, but it seemed at times they wanted to be caught. For all the talk amongst crime nerds about the brilliance of the Hannibal Lectors in the world, murderers almost always made egregious mistakes when they plied their trade.

Except here, there were multiple slayings, and they had no murder weapon, no physical evidence of a specific person, and no all-encompassing motive for the crimes. However Brandt was doing it, that fat loser guard was outsmarting the whole department.

Worse, Dani had never been one to believe in faeries or evil, and in fact, she was something for a stickler for the deliberative method, which meant she knew that something always caused something else in a consecutive manner—

without otherworldly superstition or psychobabble to interfere with irrefutable facts and logic.

Problem was, these events had jarred those long-forgotten memories of Everson from Dani's mind, and now she had the peculiar sensation she was dealing with a similar and unknowable cause. It wasn't something she could put into writing or would even want to if she wanted to keep her job, but her intuition was telling her she better pay attention to this odd sense of unnaturalness if she was to have any hope of solving the case.

Besides, if they didn't find something soon, Brandt was gonna keep on stacking up the bodies, and that prospect was simply unacceptable. Whatever her understanding of the details, Dani knew saving lives here meant she had better figure out her opponent's secrets. What those secrets were might be difficult to discover, but the answer was always there if she was willing to keep looking. And Dani was always willing.

Stepping closer to Dani, Hideo shook his head and woke her from her worried thoughts. "We have zero physical evidence against Brandt. And you know we've had him tailed since the first killing. His phone and messages have been tapped—and still nothing."

Nodding, Dani thought for a moment before coming to a decision. "True…but how do you get someone to fight when you know they want to avoid confrontation?"

Unsure, Hideo raised his eyebrows in response.

"You provoke them," said Dani, answering her own question. "Mess with people they care about. Force them to make mistakes…and then we can stop that sick fucker in his tracks."

Chapter Sixteen

Terry's less-than-impressive sedan swung into a visitor's parking space next to a series of potted plants lining the front of several attractive residential buildings. The other spaces near him were populated by pricy vehicles, all of which were of a considerably better vintage than the dilapidated cars in his much cheaper apartment complex.

Here, the environment was also quieter, without the loud music or loitering tough guys that were such common features of the communal area in Terry's hardscrabble community.

Daytime was waning, but plenty of light was still available in the leafy confines of the residential condo association. Automatic lights from a brace of lamp posts had yet to be started from their nighttime timers, and residents of the area did not look in a hurry as they took walks in the cooler temperatures of the ebbing sunlight.

Swinging his feet out of the car, Terry righted himself and looked down at his small bouquet of flowers. He hadn't brought the expensive kind on this occasion, but at least Emma would know he was thinking of her. It was important for a girl to know her man cared about her, and Terry had decided that each time he visited her, he would make her feel special—it's what gentlemen did.

Moving next to some other vehicles, Terry looked down at his image in the glass of a side window of a shiny green BMW. Looking spiffy, clean, and dressed in a pair of slacks and a white dress shirt, he smoothed over a cowlick in his recently trimmed hair and smiled in self-satisfaction. Such was his recent run of good luck that he felt positively vibrant and contented with the world, a feeling he hadn't had in…well, ever.

As Terry light-stepped toward Emma's apartment, he encountered a couple pushing twins in a dual-baby stroller, and he imagined that could be his own life at some point in the future. He had never thought of himself as the fatherly type, but with the way things were going, why wouldn't he want to make that happen? With a good woman at his side and his games to run in his free time, the sky was the limit for his formerly limited lifestyle possibilities. Terry smiled at the young couple, an overweight and seemingly kind pair, with an affectionate expression, and in his mind, he superimposed his own image into their relaxing late-afternoon stroll.

As he moved closer to the door, Terry abruptly felt the gnawing sense of dread he often felt, that same feeling of worry and angst he had experienced his whole life in dealing with women. Stopping, he tried to push his self-doubt aside. Like always, he wrestled with his inability to have real relationships with females, as it seemed to him they were a baffling species who would always be unknowable to an everyday guy like himself.

It wasn't just that Terry didn't place a high value on his physical appearance and so was unappealing to girls, it was also his sense that women could never understand his particular needs. His strange habits, the father that would always be a part of his life, his…games, his poor work prospects, all these things conspired to make ladies seem like they could never appreciate him. And that was fair, because Terry knew inside that the vast majority would never want to appreciate him.

The problem with this lack of success with females, of course, was that the fairer sex continued to look so damn good. Whatever control he exerted over the rest of his life, he couldn't deny the fact that he needed to hold and touch a woman, and not just the streetwalkers he sometimes visited in the bad part of Sacramento when he felt particularly lonely.

No, Terry needed the real thing, and with Emma, he knew he was on the cusp of something special, something that would lead to an extended relationship like other normal people had. He had waited for this his whole life, and now he just had to follow his instincts to make the unimaginable happen.

Overcoming his insecurity, Terry shook his head, pasted a smile on his face, and knocked firmly on the door. He forced a relaxed expression onto his face while he waited, even as he ground his jaw in awkward anticipation.

It didn't take long for an answer, and the door was flung open by Emma. She stood in the well-lit doorway, her eyes fixed on Terry with a cool look, one that wasn't kind or hopeful. She was dressed in sweatpants and a loose shirt, and no makeup or attempt to look presentable was evident on her disinterested face.

"Am I too early?" asked Terry, his forced smile melting away. "The movie starts in thirty minutes…is something wrong?"

Emma looked down at his yet-to-be-presented flowers and frowned. "Terry, I think we need to think things through here. I'm not really able to get involved with anybody right now."

"Wh…what?" stammered Terry. "Did I do something wrong? I thought…"

Shaking her head, Emma made a passing attempt at trying to be gentle. "It's not you. I just need to keep to myself for now. I wish you good luck…with your life."

"But…I don't understand. You…we were having such a good—."

Emma began closing the door, ending the conversation in a curt manner. Overwhelmed by the sudden twist of events, Terry pushed his flowers in the way, preventing it from shutting. His eyes grew desperate as he leaned in, and his pathetic expression was imploring as he tried to meet her gaze through the crack in the door and frame.

"Terry, get back from the door, now," shouted Emma, pushing the bouquet outside and wrenching the door shut. Calling from the other side of the barrier, her muffled tone was decidedly less kind. "If you come back, I'll call the police. And don't even think about coming to my job—I carry a gun everywhere."

Mortified, Terry didn't know what to say. With his chin quivering, tears beaded in his eyes, and he scanned the door, like he was considering how he could get through it. As the moments dragged on, his formerly happy features turned to those of a blubbering and distraught boy.

As Terry's trembling hand reached toward the door to knock again, to somehow talk some sense into Emma, he heard a man clearing his throat behind him. Spinning around, Terry's wide eyes became fearful as he took in the sight of a witness to this horrific rejection.

A large black man, tall and muscular, stood there with his eyes locked on Terry. Dressed in a tight-fitting and bland security uniform, this was not the figure of someone who did this work due to weak job prospects. Instead, he looked like he could wrestle a bear—and win.

Shaking his head with an unhidden warning, the man spoke with a Jamaican accent. "It isn't worth it, my man. You should leave, and now, to avoid any…unpleasantries."

Shocked, Terry had no idea what to do. Thinking over his options, he realized he had none. As he lowered his shamed eyes, Terry walked away from the apartment, making sure to avoid meeting the gazes of the guard or any of the numerous residents who had noticed the developing disturbance in the quiet complex.

Dropping his flowers in a trash receptacle attached to a post, Terry stumbled over to his car. As he slid into the front seat with a grunt, he was now different than before, and all the joy had left his formerly hopeful face. Peering into his rearview mirror, he focused deeply into his own eyes.

Terry's demeanor was sharply embarrassed, with equal measures of self-pity, mournful sadness, and now... burgeoning rage. His formerly innocuous face, the one that recently housed the budding expectations and worries of a normal guy looking for a way to be happy, was now replaced by a vengeful and focused hatred.

Starting his car, Terry bit down the clawing anger that rose within his guts. Like a suddenly committed and aggressive predator, he now knew there was no delusion of normalcy to be had in his life, and the wheels of manic anger turned sharply towards a future where no limitations would deny him his justice.

Huffing in deep breaths, Terry kept his gaze straight ahead and pondered his next moves with unrelenting rage. Jerking his car in reverse, he wrenched the wheel and turned the car out of the lot with little regard to traffic as he accelerated away from the complex.

Several cars honked at his chaotic maneuver, and one hand shot out the side of a passing Tesla to flip a finger at his inconsiderate driving skills. Undaunted, Terry pressed the gas pedal to the floor, moving his feeble car as fast as possible to put as much space between his recent shame and a future that would disregard all his prior considerations of living a normal life.

The slight whine of his car's timing belt was the only sound to announce the goodbye to yet another failed love interest.

#

Driving through a middle-class neighborhood of cracked-pavement streets and uneven sidewalks, Hideo edged gently around groups of playing kids and their harried parents. With a large plastic soda cup in his hand, one of the types that allowed the consumption of a day's calories in one slurping session, he met the gaze of each pedestrian who looked his way. Always one to show a broad and engaging smile, Hideo grinned with enthusiasm at the assorted people he drove past.

Outside, early nighttime had replaced the lighted sky, and the residential area was filled with post-work and post-school families ending their busy days with a last stroll before retiring for the night. The lighthearted mood of the neighborhood was infectious, with everything in order for an enjoyable end to the community's daily routine.

To Hideo's side sat Dani, and she also looked upon the local scene with an approving grin. Dani had never had the urge to be a mother because, after looking deep inside herself, she never had felt a maternal instinct, and she didn't feel like inflicting her sometimes-cynical worldview on another human being, particularly if it was to be her own. She also knew she was selfish because kids usually took all the time of every parent friend she ever had, and it was more socially acceptable to say *I don't have the instinct for it* than to admit *the little brats will take all my time and keep me from having fun.*

Still, she did love sharing time with happy kids, as they seemed to make the world a better place with their irresistible smiles and ravenous appetites for fun. Who could not love watching children playing and facing the world with unbridled joy as they went about their innocent lives? *As long as they're someone else's responsibility, they're the perfect creatures.*

Holding up her mobile phone, Dani speed-dialed a number and tapped the speaker function to enable a hands-free conversation.

Alone in his room, Terry sat near his desktop computer, watching a program with shambling zombies and idiotic characters doing things no sane person would actually do during the apocalypse.

It seemed to Terry that such programs were the height of stupidity because, if he had the chance to live through such a world-ending event, it should actually be easy to survive. If you could find some like-minded people, it wouldn't be difficult to move to a small town and live the good life, or at least a calm life away from the hordes. It's not like dead creatures would know you had moved to Yellowstone and try to use a map to find you.

Also, if there were only a few hundred thousand people alive in the world, then the collected MREs from the military and canned goods from civilian society would last for decades. So why did the survivors always act like they were one step from starvation?

And why was it so hard to imagine that survivors would actually be nice to each other? If the end of the world came with obviously impossible zombies taking over, Terry thought that people would probably be a little more introspective about the afterlife. If unbreathing corpses were roaming around by the millions, then whoever remained alive no longer had to worry about being atheists. How dumb would it be to act like nothing had changed afterwards?

And why were there always biker groups that thrived after society had collapsed? Wouldn't people want to stay in vehicles that protected them from the bites of the dead dudes? It's not like tattoos and loud Harleys would make it easier to avoid being eaten.

Of course, from a survival standpoint, all bets were off if the zombies were the fast-running variety, like in the remake of *Dawn of the Dead* from the early 2000s. Those fuckers would kill you quickly, especially if you needed to shoot them in the head to bring them down. Terry was no gun fanatic, but he had shot often enough to know hitting something in the head that was moving was next to impossible. He himself had a hard enough time punching holes in the stationary targets in their midsections, so he understood he would quickly succumb to the maws of the undead if his survival depended on headshots.

Terry's attention was suddenly caught by his phone from atop his desk, where the cracked screen showed an incoming call from a "Private Number."

Annoyed at the interruption of his important night of zombie movies, he dropped his headset to the side and answered. "Yeah, who is this?"

"Terry?" asked Dani, and she motioned for Hideo to stay quiet. "How are you doing? Haven't heard from you since…never."

Terry frowned at the phone, lowering his voice to almost a whisper. "Who's this?"

"It's Detective Isaksson. My partner and I visited you a while back, at your work. When you had some kind of pizza accident?"

Some time passed, and Terry licked his lips nervously.

"You still there? Feeling shy?"

"What do you want?" replied Terry, not sounding happy for the opportunity to chat.

"What I really want is for you to confess to the murders you've committed, but I won't hold my breath."

More silence followed, with both Dani and Hideo noticing Terry didn't deny the open accusation.

Finally, one came. "You're harassing me. I haven't hurt anyone."

"Right, you can go with that for now," Dani said, keeping a sarcastic tone. "We found the poison in the lawyer you had murdered. I should say 'assassinated,' because whoever did it was certainly that."

"Certainly what?" asked Terry, and he moved his eyes around the room, as if looking for something. His gaze fell on a small figure set above an alarm clock on a shelf. The little character was dressed in black leather and had a small knife used for killing its victims when they didn't see it coming.

"An assassin," responded Dani. "Our lab still can't figure out what kind of poison killed the attorney. That's very clever of you. Congrats."

"You're…nuts."

Dani grinned over at Hideo before continuing, flashing an expression that said *watch this*. "Thanks, that's quite a compliment. But we'll also figure out why you killed the steroid freak. What did he do to deserve that? Make fun of you?"

Annoyed, Terry raised his voice. "What…are you talking about?"

"Yes, keep playing dumb, Terry. Anyway, that was the past. Let's talk about the present. Specifically, your present. And…your relationships."

Terry leaned into the phone. His doughy appearance was confused, then worried. "My relationships?"

Dani's voice grew overtly amused, and she let the question hang in the air for a moment before replying. "It's bad form to answer questions with your own question. Please try to follow me here. How is your girlfriend, Emma?"

Terry's grip on his phone tightened, and his breaths grew heavy. Still, he remained quiet.

"We had a conversation with her," said Dani, letting some amusement leak into her words. "We thought she should know about your history of stalking…and restraining orders."

Speaking between clenched teeth, Terry protested in a low voice. "I've never been charged with a crime. Ever."

"Well, not yet, you haven't. Still, it's funny how someone loses romantic interest when they find their suitor is a psychopath. I don't think you'll be getting any Christmas cards from her any time soon."

From the driver's seat, Hideo looked over and met Dani's gaze. He nodded at his partner in admiration, as if to say *good one.*

Dani grinned and continued the remote conversation. "And then there were your wealthy geek benefactors from their weekend game: Randall, Sanders, and Jacobs?"

Terry's eyes grew wide. "What did you…?"

"They were surprised you had these things in you, Terry. But I think your gig with them has now come to an end. In fact, Randall said, and I quote, 'That crazy fucker needs to burn.' I would suppose that means you've been disinvited from further games. Hope you didn't need all that tax-free cash. It's all gone."

Frustrated, Terry's face flushed with anger. "You fucking bitch. I'll…"

Biting off his words, Terry went silent. Running one hand through his hair, his thoughts ran into raw panic, and emotionally he felt like the earth itself was collapsing below him into an eternal pit.

"That's the guy I wanted to talk to—the real Terry Brandt, the sick, evil, murdering one. Everywhere you go, we'll be on you, big boy. Everyone you know will suspect or ignore you. That's the price for what you've been doing. But…if you want to be a real man for once in your pathetic life and come clean, we'd be happy—."

Terry hung the phone up and tossed it on the bed. Standing, he paced in his room, shaking with rage. His features were barely recognizable as he stewed in his anger, and his flitting eyes moved to his stack of books and figures on a table next to his bed.

In the detectives' car, Dani looked down at her phone to ensure the connection was broken. Peering up at Hideo, she grinned and spoke in a hopeful voice. "Well, that went well. Now, let's see what he does."

#

Walking into the kitchen area, Terry wore a grungy robe and socks filled with holes. His demeanor was off, with his face showing a strange mixture of irritation and silent hostility. As he paced to the refrigerator, he passed his father at the kitchen table, who looked up in surprise at being ignored.

Wayne sat hunched over a stack of papers, and looking down from his son, he scrunched his face up and filled in some information in one of the columns. Next to his paperwork sat a soda can and a bag of chocolate candy, and next to his snack was the kitten Terry had given him, playing on the tabletop with some string Wayne had found in an old shoe box in his closet. Sticking his fingers into the kitten's belly, he absently toyed with the feline while filling out one of the forms.

Terry turned from the fridge and held up his own soda, which he sipped at for some time while watching his father. Duly occupied with his writing, Wayne continued his work for several minutes as Terry peered at him.

Finally setting aside his pen, Wayne ran a hand over his sober face and looked up. "I…umm, took your advice. Went down and got an application from that company."

Nodding, Terry didn't respond. Instead, he returned to the refrigerator and took out some lunch meat and cheese. Reaching into a cupboard, he retrieved a loaf of bread and commenced making a thick sandwich.

Disturbed by the silence, Wayne spoke louder and gestured to the kitten. "I also wanted to say…thanks for the cat. He seems like a good one."

Finishing his sandwich preparation, Terry nodded again at his father. There was no cheer or kindness in his eyes as he stared at the small cat. "Cats are good pets. They're easy to care for and usually fun to have around. Only problem is they aren't much for loyalty."

Chuckling, Wayne agreed with a considered nod. "True…they own you, instead of the other way around."

Chewing on his dry sandwich, Terry approached Wayne. Breaking off a piece of ham, he offered it to the kitten by setting it on the table. True to form, the animal abandoned playing with Wayne and attacked the meat.

Walking back to the kitchen, Terry turned around and leaned against the counter. Offering Wayne a humorless smile, he spoke in a voice that was detached, like his mind was elsewhere. "Loyalty is a hell of a thing. You think someone is on your side, and BAM, they betray you. Turn against you."

Surprised, Wayne tilted his head in confusion. "Who you talkin' about?"

"Lots of people—starting with mom. I haven't ever really had anyone on my side. Since school, when all those shithead kids made fun of me…ridiculed me. I've always been on my own."

Terry's face grew icy cold, with eyes that suddenly seemed fierce and utterly ruthless. For the first time, it was Wayne that looked away, unwilling to hold his son's gaze.

"Of course," Terry continued, "there are those that support the traitors. They're no better."

Standing straight, Terry walked to the living room, where he motioned out the sliding-glass door to the wider world. "Just like in the real word. Corporations, special interests, even the government. They all screw you over. While they take what they want and line their pockets, the little man gets nothing."

Wayne snorted in agreement. "Can't fucking argue with that. Seen it my whole life."

Smiling distantly, Terry moved to the kitchen table. As he got close, his eyes grew eager, like he was motivated by something new and was now ready to set out in a new direction. His features became enthusiastic as he glared down at Wayne. "I think there's finally gonna come a time when they all get what's coming to them. All of them. No more using us…no more free pass in persecuting those that are different…and weak."

Bewildered, Wayne returned Terry's gaze. "How does that happen? What can you do—?"

Terry interrupted his father with a raised an impatient tone. "It happens when karma finally catches up to them, Dad. When someone finally gives them a dose of their own medicine. Someone gets a little payback for all those times they looked down at us."

Raising his eyebrows, Wayne's expression grew shocked, like he was staring at a person he had never known. The son he hadn't respected in his whole life suddenly seemed so much more than he'd ever been before. This ought to have brought pride to his heart, but instead, something like dread washed across Wayne's features.

"I'm going to my room," said Terry, inclining his head towards the back of the apartment. As he stared toward his room, he thought some more, considering some frightful new direction to his life. "Gonna be there the rest of the day. Don't bother me—for anything."

Turning, Terry strode down the darkish hallway. Wayne, startled by the change in his formerly meek son, followed him with his eyes the whole way to his room. When the door clicked shut behind him, Wayne returned his troubled gaze to his job application.

Unable to keep his train of thought, Wayne dropped his pen on the table. Looking over at the kitten, he noticed the little creature continued to scarf its tasty lunch meat, oblivious to the world or any of the pressing problems in it.

Chapter Seventeen

Daylight had almost left the sky, and only a faint tinge of yellow remained to color a few wisps of visible clouds. Under the decreasing light, several stands of evergreen trees swayed under the force of a smooth westerly wind, and matched with swirling pockets of tall grass, the scattered vegetation of the valley floor whooshed with an incessant and seemingly eternal rhythm.

The broad and forceful Sacramento River flowed through these trees and brush, cutting across the dark and compacted earth of the flat ground. Being a powerful waterway that provided much-needed irrigation to the arid area, its width and depth were substantial, and the meandering current of the broad river turned over in swirling eddies on its way toward the distant Pacific Ocean.

Next to the gentle tributary's current was a picnic area, with numerous parking spots aligned to face the water, tables, and benches. Several unused barbecue grills stood near the tables, offering a peaceful place for cooking and family enjoyment in the pleasant rural environment.

A paved road ran parallel with the waterway, and a few hundred yards downstream, it twisted away from the river toward several nearby housing developments.

Carrie sat at a table that was closest to the water. Across from her was her husband Carlos, and he appeared relaxed as he glanced across the red-painted table at his flustered wife. Each wore comfortable shorts and cotton shirts, looking at ease as they enjoyed the warm summer day.

Gnawing on a spicy chicken leg, Carlos' eyes were amused as he tried to meet her gaze. On a napkin next to his other greasy hand, a further pile of stripped-free chicken bones testified to his ravenous appetite, and a half-full bucket of wings also awaited his hungry intentions.

"Every day we could sit here," Carlos said, and he wiped his prodigiously messy face on a nearby napkin before gesturing to the flowing river. "Or read, or fish...look how perfect it is. And only a few-minute walk from our back yard."

In response, Carrie tried to appear skeptical as she shook her head. "Yes, but six hundred thousand dollars? It'll take all our savings, and a third of our monthly income, assuming we BOTH are working. We'll be chained to the mortgage for the rest of our lives."

Carlos conceded the point with a reluctant nod. "True, but if we keep chasing the market, we'll never have a house. We'll still be renting when we're fifty. When we have kids, I don't want them to grow up in a condo—even a nice one."

Looking down at a brochure on the table, Carrie sighed. On the glossy front of the pamphlet, in bold lettering, was written "$10000 in upgrades for early closing!" Under the writing was a happy family of four—a father, mother, and a boy and girl—with intense smiles. The actors' faces were appropriately enthusiastic, with their bright-white teeth looking as if they were dyed daily to achieve dental perfection. The river they now sat near was nice, but it looked nothing like the glistening and perfect waterway depicted in the brochure.

Shrugging, Carrie tried not to let the prospect of such a perfect place to live take her away in the moment. Unlike Carlos, she was the calm head in the couple, but by the amused glance of her husband, she could tell he was winning the argument. Worse, he knew that he was winning, which made resistance seem all the more important if she was to keep her position as the practical one in their marriage.

"Let's think about it for a few days," said Carrie, deciding to keep fighting the losing battle. "They always count on you to give in by throwing in that 'act now' BS. As if it will be all sold out before the weekend is over."

'C'mon, Carrie. We only live once…"

Glancing down the trail that abutted the waterway, Carlos motioned to six young teens pacing up the walkway toward them. Dressed in long brown robes covering their body and faces, with their hands inserted into their sleeves, the approaching group looked a bit ridiculous in the fading light. "See, we even got a contingent of altar boys that live in the area…to keep us company. Where else could we see something like that? Maybe they'll sing for us, too."

Shrugging, Carrie waved absently at the young people and moved her gaze back down to the sales brochure. Unsure of herself and still trying to determine how they could pay for the prospective house, she opted to not respond.

As the teens came close to them, one of them suddenly fell to one knee. Making a hideous choking sound, the robed kid began to cough in a bizarre cackle, like he was trying to draw breath through a jagged and too-small windpipe.

Carlos immediately noticed, and because of his extensive emergency-services training, his face filled with concern. Standing and moving close to the boys, he raised his voice. "Are you OK? Here, get outta the way; give him some room to breathe."

Stepping into the group of youngsters, Carlos patted the wheezing kid on the back and gestured for the others to give them room. "Take it easy and breathe slowly. Did you swallow something…?"

Glancing up, Carrie got a confused look. Something about the group didn't seem right. The way the young men were closing around her husband had a distinctly predatory feel to it, like they were looking for an advantageous position on her much-taller husband. Standing from the table, a concern tugged at the back of her mind, and a sense of foreboding altered her attention toward the "kids."

Carrie carefully focused on the circling group and raised her voice in warning. "Carlos…"

With a husky grunt, one of the "boys" from the group pulled a knife from his sleeve and rammed it into the side of Carlos' head. The blade severed his ear but bounced off his skull and didn't penetrate further into his head.

"Carlos, get the fuck away from them," shouted Carried, and reaching inside her purse, she tried drawing her revolver. Because she was unready for the attack, the weapon was wedged at the bottom of her bag, and she fumbled as she tried to yank it free.

Astonished, Carlos pushed away his attacker while grabbing at his grievous head wound. Back-peddling, he tried to move away from the surrounding figures. All at once, each of the robed forms pulled out their own daggers and began to stab the off-duty cop.

Scoring several vicious hits with their slashes and stabs, Carlos began screaming in pain and surprise. Spinning around, he belatedly grabbed at his waist, trying to pull his own pistol free.

His attackers swarmed over him. Jabbing him with savage thrusts from their thick-bladed daggers, Carlos fell to the ground under the onslaught. As he tried to vainly to fight off his assailants, he held up his arms to ward off their blows. Blood sprayed from a score of wounds as they repeatedly shanked their much-larger opponent, and their vicious thrusting attacks pierced into most of his organs, making Carlos wail in agony.

His cries becoming weaker, Carlos dropped his arms, and it was almost over before it even began. The continuous *schucking* of the heavy blades into his neck, chest, and stomach continued as they pressed their ruthless advantage. Up and down their blood-coated hands stabbed, as if they were forced to kill him many times over.

Finally dragging her revolver free of her purse, Carrie aimed and fired four times, twice each, into the back of two of the boys. The crack of her rounds matched with gore blowing out the fronts of their bodies, and the stricken assailants collapsed across the convulsing figure of her mortally wounded husband.

The remaining four now turned towards Carrie, their bloody blades held up and at the ready. Strangely, the hands that held the knives were gnarled and black, like the fingers had been broken and grown back at odd angles. Moving slowly, the wicked killers advanced her way. Their faces were still covered by their hoods, and they appeared unafraid of her weapon.

Cocking her hammer and aiming carefully, Carrie shot the closest one in the face. With brains blowing out the back of his head, he collapsed to the ground, unmoving and instantly dead.

Out of ammunition, Carrie's wild eyes turned away from the remaining aggressors. Panicked and stumbling, she fled upstream on the river path, where she raised her voice into a pleading shout. "Somebody help…help me. Please."

Moving faster than her pursuers, she angled toward the river, hoping for an escape from this sudden barbarism. Picking up speed and pushing away thoughts of her beloved husband, she focused on a break in the bushes and possible safety beyond. Thinking she would get away, she silently thanked God she had trained as a runner for most of her adult life.

An arrow from behind flitted and plunged into the back of Carrie's left leg. Collapsing on the ground with a grunt, she grabbed at the meat of her calf, where a crossbow bolt had pierced all the way through it. Grabbing at the hideous wound, she vainly tried to control the blood that pumped from the hole in the muscly flesh of her exposed skin. Terrified and in horrible pain, she looked back with a panicked grimace at the three remaining attackers.

One of the figures behind her was reloading a crossbow by bracing it on the ground and pulling back on its tight string. The other two had withdrawn their own missile weapons from their robes and slowly walked toward her. They moved oddly, as if lurching from one misshapen foot to another, and their methodical and unconcerned pace appeared strange as they sized up their prey.

In agony, Carrie dragged herself to the river. Pushing into the water from her good leg, she splashed into the current and began to swim erratically. Making slow progress, she was flailing upstream from her assailants as she swam towards the middle of the cold and strong river.

Stopping on the riverbank, her diminutive attackers lined up their shots and aimed carefully. Releasing their firing triggers, the wicked metal and barbed crossbow bolts plunged into Carrie's thrashing body as she floated down toward them. Trying to turn away from the missile onslaught, she was unable to shield herself completely in the water, and the ends of the thick arrows stuck deeply into the clammy flash of her back and neck.

Reloading again, the merciless crossbowmen loosed another volley into her exposed flank. With each *thunk* of an impact, Carrie's grunts and motions for escape grew quieter. Struck by a half-dozen quarrels and unable to get away, she finally went silent and gave up her vain struggle to survive.

Rolling over and convulsing into a dreamy death pose, Carrie's body went limp, and her suddenly still corpse drifted farther down the lazy stretch of the Sacramento River. Behind her calm form, a hazy cloud of blood leaked from her body as she bled out entirely.

As her unmoving form drifted into the descending darkness, her attackers slipped their weapons back into their full robes. Apparently unworried about their crimes, they continued walking upstream, moving quietly away from the horrific and violent scene.

Behind them, with just a few rays of the sun left to illuminate the area, Carlos' dead form lay under the bodies of two of his vicious attackers. Suddenly, a breeze picked up, and the hoods on his assailants blew open to reveal the grotesque, dog-like faces of his killers.

Misshapen yellow teeth jutted from the bony and deformed jawlines of the small creatures, and protruding snouts, much like a pig but considerably more vile, adorned their abominable faces. Looking like a cross between a heinous devil and a cursed animal, the bizarre monstrosities appeared dangerous—even in death.

Abruptly, a more powerful rush of air picked up, and the monstrous assailants' bodies began to dissipate into a chalky, sand-like substance. In a few moments, the corpses of the animal-looking murderers became dust, with nothing left to indicate they, their weapons, or their clothes were ever there. As the wind swirled around them, the powdery remnants of their existence were picked up by the vigorous breeze and blown into the evening's fresh air.

The picnic area was now quiet, and only the bloody and broken form of Carlos was left in the faint light. Alone in death, he lay face-up, his shocked eyes staring up at the sky and looking at nothing in particular.

#

The small football arched through the office air before falling back out of sight with a soft *chuk*. Again, the small pigskin, adorned with the team logo of the Green Bay Packers, rose into the air, then fell down under the bright light of the staid office setting. For the better part of the minute, the ball continued its relentless motion, up and down.

Looking up from her desk, Dani compressed her lips into an irritated scowl. With her fingers paused above her keyboard, she took a deep breath in a bid for self-control. "If you don't stop that, I'm going to throw a knife at you."

Across from her, Hideo sat with his feet propped on his own desk. Clutching the ball as he prepared to throw it up again, he flashed an innocent smile. Motioning to Dani's sandwich and mix of cheese and lunch meats on a plate next to her, where a simple knife was also arranged with a glob of butter on it, he spoke in a matter-of-fact tone. "You only have a butter knife, so it isn't likely you'd get a killing blow. Besides, this helps me think."

Dani chuckled and shook her head. "You need to think harder, then, before the rest of the town gets killed. I took this job to avoid the big-city crime of the larger departments, but now it's looking like corpse-central."

"Yeah, this isn't good, and that's putting it mildly. An off-duty uniform gets knifed by the river, and his wife is missing. Maybe it was something in the water, literally? Some kind of rampaging mermaid?"

Dani tilted her head in disapproval at Hideo's dark humor, then ran through the town's recent violent events in her frustrated thoughts. "What are the chances it's our guy?"

"No chance at all. We got the nerd's apartment under surveillance, and his cell is monitored. Same with his social media accounts and apps. No way he can communicate with anyone. Unless he's found a way to communicate to some zombie assassins by clairvoyance, it's a dead-end…pardon the pun."

Reclining in her chair, Dani crossed her arms, looking unconvinced. "Yeah…but this makes me think about all the times people say things can't be done, then people do them anyway. For instance, think of the song 'Achy Breaky Heart.' At some point, someone wrote that tune, and someone else said it would never be a hit. If the writer hadn't kept doing his thing, we would've never been able to experience Billy Ray's audible masterpiece."

Hideo grinned a broad and contemptuous smile, one that showed his lack of love for the music mentioned. Becoming contemplative, he prepared to throw the football again but stopped when Dani's threatening hand crept towards her knife. Lowering his voice, his earnest eyes became serious. "OK, then what's our play? We can't sit here and do nothing, and we can't bring Brandt in with zero evidence."

Dani sighed and plucked her slice of bread from the desktop. Reaching over, she laid several slices of cheese over the butter-topped and open-faced sandwich. Holding it up, she chewed on her lip and focused on the food for several moments as she prepared to take a bite. "Alright, let's do this. You go talk to the deceased cop's family, friends, whoever.

Find a connection to the other murders. There's got to be something there. Meanwhile…I'll go find some other way to kick the hornet's nest."

Nodding, Hideo laid the ball aside and stood from his desk. Grabbing his coat from his chair, he stopped to inspect an indeterminate food stain on the black-colored front of the heavy suede jacket. Wrinkling his nose, he put the coat on before speaking in a sober voice. "Be careful, Dani. We now got bodies of completely unconnected and innocent people here. On the other hand, we are involved, and Brandt knows us by name and face. If he's offing random cops at the river, I doubt he's worried about adding one or both of us to his list of victims."

Dani thought over Hideo's foreboding words, and the strength of the threat Terry represented became clearer in her mind. Setting her food aside, she refrained from eating, having for the moment lost her appetite. Rising and getting her own coat, she motioned to the window outside as she also got ready to leave. Her features were a mix of determination and soft dread as she spoke. "They may be innocent, but they're not unconnected. We just need to find the 'why,' and the 'how' will follow."

Dani took a deep breath, and her normally playful features became more grave and worried. "I hope."

Chapter Eighteen

The parking lot of the large supermarket was largely empty at this time of the late afternoon. A few cars filled the spaces near several small shops to the side of the large grocery store, chief among them a too-cramped cafe and a seemingly abandoned pet store with a few interested customers staring at puppies through its front window.

Farther from the strip-mall businesses, some pedestrians walked by on an adjoining sidewalk that ran the length of a busy road filled with whooshing cars and sputtering pickup trucks.

The glare from the descending sun cast an eye-squinting glow from the window of the food store, and several signs were pasted to the front glass announcing "Papayas," "Bananas," and "Yes, Vegan Supplies Available!" Farther down the window were advertisements for various liquors, with "Vodka

2 Bottles/22.99" being the most attractive and prominent booze on offer.

Wayne stood in front of that sign, and he wore a stretched white t-shirt and tattered hat with a long-faded insignia of John Deere above its weathered and bent brim. Licking his lips at the alcohol for sale, he stood there for some time as he contemplated the bang for the buck it offered, as well as how much he could afford to buy now.

Wayne realized the best use of his funds would be to get more volume when he bought—the bastards always counted on you not needing a huge bottle, and then you had to come back later and buy the smaller bottle again. Why not just get what you needed now, instead of worrying about running out at some point late at night, right when he most needed that end-of-the-night buzz?

He knew the answer to that, of course. If Wayne loaded up on too much drink, he wouldn't have enough cash to buy dope later, and it always seemed that Hal from his old job was charging more and more each time Wayne wanted to get stoned. He knew he really should get a new supplier for his marijuana habit, but as much as he hated Hal's prices, he did offer a good product. There was always something to be said for paying for higher-quality pot, whatever your financial limitations.

Sighing, Wayne realized a working man like himself was always going to struggle with such thoughts: it was one or the other these days, and the dollar never seemed to stretch as far as it had in the past. It wasn't really fair that he spent most of his life working—that is, when he wasn't fired for one reason or another—and yet never could quite afford to get the quality products he needed at the right price.

Looking like a man on a mission, Wayne inhaled a deep breath and strode to the broad entrance of the neighborhood store. With a whoosh of the automatic doors and the greeting of the almost too-cool air inside, he stared with purpose as he paced ahead.

The first order of business was to get a cart, and reaching to the side, Wayne pulled out a good-sized one from a brace of metal shopping baskets in a cordoned-off area. He pushed it for several yards before realizing its front right wheel pointed to the side and rattled, meaning that for the millionth time in his life, he managed to choose the crappiest shopping cart available.

Shaking his head at his eternally bad luck, Wayne walked with determination, passing by a few old people shopping and some stockers loading up a display of salsa and chips. Paying them no mind, he focused to the back aisle of the store, where rows of wine and other discolored bottles offered him a wondrous choice of intoxicants for the long night ahead.

Arriving at his treasured destination, Wayne let his eyes wander across the collections of cheap wine and industrial-sized spirits. Pushing his squeaky cart forward, his attention fell on a display of red wine that stood next to a mass of white-bottled vodka.

Leaning down, Wayne grabbed a bottle of vodka, but as he put it into his basket, his precise focus turned to the blood-red wine in the prominent display to his side. It was always so hard to choose what would be best for him when he worked through the possibilities of his daily encounters with his alcoholic inclinations. He had always had a hard time deciding such things, and the choice could make him positively frustrated at times. Truth was, he had been toying with the idea of laying off the bottle for a while, but old habits died hard when it was the only thing he really enjoyed in his sorry life.

Looking close at the wine, he let his fingers brush across the label that offered *Merlot* as an enticing counterpoint to his original drinking intentions. Vodka had seemed like the perfect indulgence for the weekend, but he had read somewhere that red wine could even be good for the health…so, maybe he should get that instead? *Decisions, decisions…*

Becoming more and more uncertain, Wayne pondered his course of action for a considerable time, assuming a far-off gaze as he stood still.

"I'd go for the wine. You can really make the moment last with some vino."

Surprised, Wayne turned to gaze at Dani, whom he hadn't noticed up until now. She must have appeared from the far end of the aisle, but shit, she had really sneaked up on him. "Who are you?"

Dani offered Wayne a fake smile. "I'm a friend of your son's. I'm glad I ran into you."

Dani extended her hand, but Wayne wasn't interested in shaking. He fixated on her smart-aleck expression and shook his head doubtfully. "No, you ain't. He would've told me about you—whoever the fuck you are."

Dani perked her eyebrows at the foul language but wasn't surprised at the attitude. She interrogated him with her eyes, mulling over his asshole demeanor for several prolonged moments. Almost apologetically, she flashed her detective's badge. "Caught me…Mr. Brandt."

"What do ya want?" asked Wayne, and his unsmiling and suspicious features continued their guarded glare.

"I wanted to talk about your son…and about what he's doing with his life, as well as other people's."

Wayne's steely stare didn't diminish. "I'm listening."

Dani stepped near Wayne, and his expression grew surprised as she leaned in close, far closer than he had expected. Only inches from his face, she lowered her voice so only he could hear. "We think Terry is connected to multiple homicides. We think he's killing people he doesn't like."

Dani let those words linger in the air, and her inquisitive eyes took in Wayne's confused emotions from his scraggly face and antagonistic bearing. He looked shocked for a moment, but then appeared less so as he processed her accusation. Like a baffled child that had just put together an answer to a perplexing math problem, he seemed to piece together something from his scattered thoughts and memories.

"Terry wouldn't hurt anyone. You're full of shit, cuz' he'd be in jail if you could prove anything," said Wayne, overcoming his surprise but not appearing convinced of his own words.

"When we get all the evidence, he will be. And anyone hiding his crimes or involved in any way will be joining him. I just wanted to see what you had to say about that, Mr. Brandt. I thought maybe, if there was something to say, I'd give you a chance to speak up."

Wayne's expression grew angry, and for a second, Dani thought the older man might try to get violent. It appeared Terry's temper may have had a source in something other than a loser's frustration at his lowly position in life. Maybe his anger and rage were based on his upbringing around this grizzled bit of spiteful humanity.

Dani took a step back and cocked her head expectantly, but Wayne soon overcame his emotions and reverted to a poker face.

Wayne's sour expression oozed hostility, and he contorted his defiant face into a hostile grin. "Then go and get your evidence, ya smartass bitch. But leave me alone from now on…if you wanna talk again, then fuck off, 'cuz I ain't interested."

Taking in his words, Dani pursed her lips and kept Wayne's stare in a thoughtful pose. Nodding slowly, she offered an insincere smile to the elder Brandt, then turned reluctantly and walked away.

Wayne stared after her as she left, watching her disappear around the corner at the last aisle near the brightly lit front of the store. When she was out of sight, he squinted his eyes, working through what any of this shitty conversation could have meant.

Wayne was no Einstein and no saint, but neither was he a rat, especially with family. He'd die before telling that bitch anything to incriminate Terry. He never learned much in his life, but he knew the one quality he had in abundance relating to his only son: loyalty, at least as it pertained to the cops. He might not think much of Terry, but he thought even less about everyone else in the world. *Whatever Terry did, they must've had it comin'.*

Turning back around, Wayne resumed looking at the wine. Shrugging, he picked up and placed the dark bottle in the cart. After another moment of hesitation, he grabbed a second bottle of vodka and added that to his growing shopping collection.

#

Badger stood behind the comic store's cluttered counter with an expansive smile on his face. Holding up a large, boxed game that read *Dwarven Citadels*, he carefully read the price on a sticker underneath, then tapped that number into the cash register with several authoritative beeps.

Looking down, Badger focused on the face of a 12-year-old boy, a youngster with thick glasses and an expectant smile. Grinning, the boy held up a wad of crumpled cash and stared longingly at his soon-to-be-owned board game. Much like an impatient youth who was soon to adopt a cherished pet, he could barely contain his eagerness as he waited to take possession.

Badger took the money and counted out the lad's change, all the while seeing himself in the earnest kid. Looking like a proud grandfather, he bagged up the purchase and slid the package across the counter to the boy.

"Now, make sure you keep track of the hit point totals when you set up your battle," said Badger, using a sage-like tone, like that of an ancient and wise philosopher. "Nothing's more important than making sure it's a fair fight during the main siege with the ogres. They aren't just gonna let you win without a fight."

The boy nodded intensely, taking in the advice with wide eyes and bated breath.

Motioning to the front of the store, Badger moved to open the door for the boy on the way out. In his mind, nothing was more important than good customer service, especially when he had just sold an out-of-date game at a three hundred percent markup.

As Badger got close to the door, it was pulled open from the outside, and the happy kid spilled onto the sidewalk and made his way over towards his mom's waiting white SUV, all the while struggling to keep the large purchase in his arms.

Still grinning, Badger watched the young man climb into the idling vehicle, then moved his gaze to the polite visitor to his side. He was surprised to see that it was Dani who still held the door ajar.

His smile fading, Badger met her eyes, and his good mood became subdued for the first time of the day. His lack of enthusiasm was unmistakable as he greeted her dryly. "How can I help you, Detective?"

#

Minutes later, Badger and Dani stood inside, in front of the store's main display case. Under the bright light of a specially focused powerful lamp, more than one hundred figures, from horrific vampires to armored soldiers with enormous swords, were represented in the mock field of battle below them.

Usually, Badger was proud to show his varied playthings, but now there was a pallid frown occupying his worried features. "I change the monster races and fighter classes of these as often as I can—when I can get time to paint the new figures. It keeps things interesting for the kids because they come back often, and sometimes they don't have any money. They just like to look."

Nodding, Dani showed Badger an approving smile before getting down to business. "What I need to know is: what exactly has Brandt purchased in the past? And, what those figures could or would do if they were real?"

Looking puzzled, Badger rubbed his hand in his unkempt hair, then scratched his scalp in confusion. "If they were real?"

"Just humor me."

"O…kay. I already told you he picked up a wizard a few days ago," Badger replied, twisting his features as he tried to retrieve his specific memories. "Other than that, I'm not sure what else he bought. These things come in loads of configurations and poses."

The empty store went silent as Dani thought over the problem. Concentrating, a light went on in her eyes, and she clicked her tongue in a *Eureka* moment. Taking out her mobile phone, she thumbed through several screens.

Coming to the photo Dani took the night she first interviewed Brandt at his security guard job, she handed it to Badger. "What about those? There are more on the next screens."

Interested, Badger focused down at the screen. Pointing at the original axe-wielding figure, he spoke admiringly. "The first is a Half-Orc fighter. He's a 'tank,' which means he can really deal out and absorb the damage that a party usually faces when fighting. You always put him in front, so your weaker members don't get killed right away."

Flicking to the next photo, Badger nodded. "Those are goblins. Nasty buggers. They use numbers to overwhelm you, but they're pretty easy to kill. You might have like twenty at a time attack a party of five or six. They're a staple of any good night of creature battles."

Moving to the next screen, Badger smiled as if his eyes had just fallen on an old and reliable friend. Clearly, this character was a favorite of the store owner. "Here you got a monk. At higher levels, they can really kick ass. They're so deadly at their craft that they almost never use weapons. Imagine Bruce Lee—but with ten times the ability to attack and maim you."

Moving to the final picture, Badger squinted down. Appearing unsure, he was trying to figure out what the image of a dead-looking but very much alive and vicious figure was. Dani stepped close to get a better look at the screen.

"This looks like a ghoul…" said Badger, biting his lip and concentrating.

"That's a zombie, right?"

Badger shook his head. "Worse. Undead, like zombies, but faster and stronger. They can also be smart, too, so you gotta watch out for any nefarious traps with them. They can ambush you out of nowhere. Like… BOOM, and you're dead before you know it. I love using them as bad guys at night—when visibility is limited."

Keeping her tone low, Dani gestured out the window to the whole world beyond. "Who would play these characters in the real world, assuming someone wanted to do that?"

Grimacing, Badger shook his head. His formerly intimidated expression melted into exasperation, like he was no longer sure of Dani's mental state. "Someone…who's crazy. The only group I know are those dudes out in——."

"I looked into that, and it's definitely not them. Rich guys in expensive loafers driving European SUVs make bad acolytes. You might notice that Jim Jones' followers in South America were not exactly the elite in society. Drinking the literal Kool-Aid requires people that are searching for direction in life—not counting their seven-digit 401K balances."

It was quiet for a moment, and Badger finally shrugged and adopted an uncertain voice. "Then I don't know what's going on. Unless…you got real monsters attacking people?"

Badger flashed a smile, one that he often used to point out the ridiculous when dealing in a world of make-believe and monsters. Obviously joking, his smirk indicated his statement was self-evidently hilarious and absurd.

Returning his gaze, Dani didn't smile, and contrary to her normal attitude, she found nothing to be amused about.

Chapter Nineteen

Terry's bedroom was dark and quiet in the early night. Outside, light from nearby lights leaked through the room's windows, throwing some illumination across a table full of his game books and other assorted play figures situated near his desk.

From far in the night, a dog barked incessantly, and an angry voice screamed at the animal to "shut the fuck up" in a burst of rage at its howling.

Sitting at his computer desk, Terry breathed deeply. To the side, his bed was made, and the room looked oddly clean when compared to its disheveled and dumpy resident, like he had spent time making sure everything was in some semblance of order but had not worried about his own appearance.

From cheap computer speakers arranged next to a large computer monitor, strange-sounding Gaelic music played quietly. Sounding a bit like a combination of leprechaun tunes mixed with a religious backdrop, the odd combination somehow added a bizarre sense of dread to the otherwise calm room.

Looking down, Terry adjusted his pale desk lamp to shine more light on the desktop. On the scratched and cheap laminate surface stood an odd-looking wizard, one that had a flowing white beard and pointy ears. The fantasy-inspired figure had a dark-skinned, peculiar face recessed behind its immense beard, and its eyes seemed to shine an off-white color, as if they were emitting their own source of illumination from within its molded-metal confines.

Picking up the Elven wizard, Terry extended his hand and used a small brush to dab a last strip of paint onto its flowing green robe. The mix of colors on the figure was striking, with multiple dark shades beaming in symmetry from various layers of what looked almost like real clothing.

Sighing, Terry appeared contented with the work. Having finished the paint job, the image of the magic figure seemed positively lifelike, as if it had been crafted whole from a living and breathing person.

Turning the figure over in his hand, Terry set the brush aside and focused on its eyes. Looking intently into the miniature face, he moved the wizard back to the table. Trying to relax, he blew gently on the paint, waiting for it to dry and assume his desired shade of color.

Looking up at his computer monitor, Terry tapped the keyboard to bring the screen alive, and the computer browser before him lit up with a top-down map image of the Bay Area in Northern California. The sprawling map showed all the contours of the land, and although this specific map was only updated occasionally, it filled out the real-world outlines of the extended area, making it easy to see which location interested him.

Using his mouse to zoom in on an area northeast of San Francisco, he licked his lips several times in expectation. His normally expressive face lost all its emotion, and he took on the appearance of a disinterested observer of some unknown and faraway event.

For some time, the room remained quiet, and even the distant barks of his neighbor's loud dog came to a stop. The intensity of the moment continued, almost as if the air itself was waiting for something to happen.

Collecting himself, Terry moved his *Monster Compendium* book next to his make-believe elf. Leaning back, he stretched his back and gripped the edges of the desk. Bringing his breathing under tight control, he stared at the figure for several minutes.

In time, sweat formed on his face, and as Terry's obsessive eyes continued their malignant stare at his painted figure, his mind and thoughts drifted somewhere else.

#

The moon hung low over the dark grape orchards of the Napa Valley, and a misty fog swirled intermittently through the area that was notable for being one of the most productive wine regions in the world. In the distance, rolling hills intermingled with flat plains that were laced with yet more rows of grapes, giving the agricultural area a broad and unending feel.

From around the hilly country, the loud chirps of crickets provided an energetic backdrop to the rural environment, ensuring a staccato reminder of the closeness of nature. Above, the sky was cloudless, and the moon was immaculate and striking, providing extensive lighting for the remote and well-tended fields.

Closer in, where a two-lane highway ran next to the never-ending grape fields, a beautiful ranch house stood on a small knoll. A heavy gate and extravagant wrought-iron fence protected the property's perimeter from easy access, and from that gate, an asphalt road ran through manicured lawns toward a large, detached garage near the house. The large size of the parking building, set aside and back from the sprawling residence, meant it could house many vehicles in its spacious interior.

Constructed of heavy timbers with white supporting beams, the lengthy front porch of the home was clean and adorned with benches and furniture. It was empty now, but during daylight hours a person could spend the day resting while overlooking the gorgeous wine-growing tracts beyond it.

With wide windows offering both a view of the deserted highway and the harvesting region behind it, the house was built to enhance the enjoyment and prestige of its occupant, allowing its resident to experience the locality's relaxing and enviable sights without worrying about unwanted visitors.

The inside of the home was similarly well-organized and clean, with a living area and several rooms appointed with nice furniture and attractive prints on the wall. In another interior room that could only be described as a man cave, several immense flat televisions filled the walls' open spaces, and a leather couch, large personal bar, and custom barstools filled out the comfortable ensemble.

Farther toward the end of the house, at a point that faced away from the empty highway, John Randall stood in the well-lit kitchen. Surrounded by clean and shiny stainless appliances, he held an ever-present glass of wine in his hand. As he stared at the dark fields outside, his contented face glowed with the moment. As a man that had seen the world and worked to ensure his accomplished place in it, he made it a point in his life to take it these brief periods slowly and enjoy every minute.

Setting down his glass, Randall moved to the dishwasher and began to load a few dishes he had used to enjoy a dinner of pasta and scallops. Not one to limit himself in any way, he rarely made his own meals, but today he had let his cook have the time off to attend to some family matter or another way down in Stockton. Scowling for a moment, he realized he already missed her cooking. Whatever his talents, having to reheat gourmet food in a microwave he barely knew how to operate meant food preparation was not among them. *I should've only given her two days off, not four. Shit.*

Sliding the dishwasher tray shut, Randall stood and looked at his phone, which was buzzing and playing a hard rock ringtone from the kitchen island. "Jerry" filled the display, and he reached over and tapped the speaker function to play the conversation out loud in the quiet kitchen.

Randall spoke to the phone, his voice incredulous. "Jer, what are we gonna do? This has been the lynchpin of my happiness…for years. This blows."

Sanders, reclining in his chair in the far-away, dark lawyer office, spoke back through his own hands-free cell phone lying on the desk. "Dude, I know. I still can't believe the Dungeon Master went bat-shit nuts. It's like he created his own horror module to play in real life."

Chuckling, Randall shook his head at the exasperating situation. "Truthfully, there was always something creepy about him. But murder? Guess you never really know anyone, but I didn't think the price for hiring the geek-genius guy was outright homicide. Guess we better get ready to lawyer up ourselves."

From the other side of the conversation, Sanders' disbelieving voice turned to the more pressing matter of their own personal considerations. "As important as people dying is…where can we get someone new to do our games? It's the only way I get to drink without Audrey bitching at me."

Continuing his light humor, Randall nodded with amused eyes. "I hear you. Guess I'll have to look around the boards for a new guy…do some interviews, whatever it takes. Funny thing is, I would've paid double to win him back if his reason for leaving wasn't serial murder."

"Yeah…I guess we can put an ad in that—."

From the wall near the refrigerator, an audible alarm sounded from a security control panel. The state-of-the-art system lit up with a series of flashing red zones on an embedded large LCD screen. The pitch of the beeping was annoying in its loudness, like it was meant to wake people from the next county over.

Moving to the panel, Randall quickly disabled the alarm with a four-digit code. Staring at the numbers that still flashed, he grimaced and directed his voice back to the phone on the counter. "Bro, I gotta go. One of those fucking deer tripped the alarm again. I'll give you a call tomorrow, and we'll find a solution to our nerd problem."

"See ya!" said Sanders, ending the call.

Walking from the kitchen, Randall stepped to a window in the living room that faced northwest—toward the far interior of the property. That was the direction of the security system's focus, and he compressed his lips in thought as he stared into the distance and set his gaze on a series of lights that had been activated by the motion alarms. Standing there for several moments, he took in the fact that more than one alarm going off was unusual, especially from an area that did not have the type of surrounding vegetation that typically drew deer and animals.

Frowning, Randall paced back to the kitchen and reached down. In the middle of a set of drawers, he placed his thumb on a small electrical pad. A clicking sound ensued, and the "drawer" slid out on its own accord.

Inside, a padded compartment held a large and exquisite revolver, along with several boxes of ammunition. Made of shiny stainless steel, it was a "Performance Center Smith and Wesson" with a 6-inch barrel in the caliber of .357 magnum. Handmade to cater to those willing to pay three times the price of a normal revolver, Randall admired the weapon for several moments before withdrawing it from its hiding spot in the personally designed gun safe inside his cabinets.

Holding the piece up, Randall flipped out the cylinder to check that it was loaded. Eight cartridges occupied the cylinder, ready for action, and he grinned and slapped it shut. Unlike the vast majority of revolvers, this model held eight rounds instead of the normal six.

This was something that made Randall happy because when he dropped twelve hundred bucks on a revolver, he never knew when the added rounds might come in handy. It was important to get the most out of such purchases—guns were the last thing you wanted to skimp on when it came to quality and performance. Having to shoot anything would be a tragedy, but needing to shoot something and having a tool that didn't function right was a far worse outcome to endure.

Reaching into another drawer, Randall withdrew a 5-cell flashlight, one that was half as long as his leg. There were newer models of much-smaller flashlights to buy, and those fancy new LED systems could shine brighter, but he kept this around because it could always be used as a bludgeoning instrument in a pinch. *You can never be too careful.*

Stepping toward the porch, Randall smiled as he pushed the door open and stepped into the darkness. As he walked into the silent night, several tall lights connected to motion sensors made the backyard erupt in plentiful illumination.

#

Moving away from the well-lit back of the house, Randall paced carefully into the peaceful night. Wearing sturdy boots, his feet trudged through the soft soil that made growing wine such a profitable venture in this stretch of moderate climate north of the San Francisco Bay region.

Grapes for wine production had first been planted in the area in the late 1830s, and the first commercial ventures had subsequently begun during the Civil War. Though this was a recent endeavor for wine—after all, regions of Italy and others had been cultivating this product for thousands of years—the quality here was considered quite good, and this allowed Californian production to continually surge up until current times. Now it seemed any celebrity worth their salt had their own winery producing substantial niche and limited production runs for the collector and specialized wine markets.

Nodding at his good fortune to both own a winery and be privy to the demand for his particular variety of products, Randall, for the millionth time in his life, realized that it wasn't enough to just make something, but you had to know for whom and at what price you were making it.

Randall had known many hard-working people in his life that failed to properly capitalize on their labor by not marketing their product towards the most beneficial ends because they didn't see this simple truth. Supply and demand were one thing, but on the demand side, there were always the bargain hunters and uncultured who would never pay for quality, and he decidedly did not want to supply his varieties of wine to them.

It took him several minutes to pick his way out to the area where the alarm had been tripped. Randall's system was supposed to be able to differentiate between animals and people that were trespassing, but he knew enough about bullshit security-system salesmen to appreciate that they had no idea how many times the twenty-thousand-dollar system would give him false alarms.

Sighing, Randall arrived at the area where two rows of LED lamps were lit up on posts above where the grape fields twisted around a corner below a small hill. To his left, a small dirt road ascended into a grove of trees atop that elevated space, where a few seasonal workers' shacks—currently empty—stood, and for the moment, he couldn't see anything that would have set off the laser motion detectors.

Stopping in the middle of the bright lights, Randall turned in a lazy circle to take in the night's vague outlines around him. A cloud of bugs buzzed and hovered above the lights, but the area was otherwise silent.

Randall always loved walking these rows in the middle of the night; it seemed to him that there was comfort to be had in standing amongst your grapes, knowing that similar people had done so for millennia as they tried to gauge the value and quality of their crop for the coming harvesting season.

But…something made him continue to spin around, as if there might be something else here with him in the moment. The hairs pricked on his neck, and for once in a long time, Randall felt something that bothered him on some primeval level in his mind. As his eyes scoured his shadowy surroundings, his vision grew more acutely aware, and some sweat on his right hand made the grip on his revolver sticky as he flexed his fingers around the slick synthetic grip.

Nothing was there, though, no matter how much his unconscious mind screamed at him to be wary. Even though Randall knew there should be no predatory animals in this region that would threaten his safety, he nevertheless gripped his weapon harder as he continued to wait for…whatever was bothering him. The area around him also seemed to wait, and the lack of any animals moving about or crickets to break the quiet increased his alertness.

Finally giving up his expectant pause, Randall shrugged and mentally castigated himself for this slide into paranoia. For a moment, it had seemed he was playing the part in some childish dream, and with a shake of his head, he turned to make his way back to his well-stocked bar and numerous televisions full of sports scores and replays from the day's football games.

As he began walking towards his home, he heard the slight sound of crunching feet coming from the road that moved up the embankment to the nearby stands of trees. The steps were gentle at first, and as they grew nearer, the shadow of a figure appeared on the dirt path above him.

Clicking on his flashlight, Randall shined the light at the incoming figure, who he could see was moving at a relaxed pace toward him from perhaps fifty yards away.

Bizarrely, the figure looked to be an old man. The stooped figure of an aged man plodded toward him in the darkness, not pausing for a moment as his pace remained constant. In his right hand, he carried a long walking stick as he pressed forward, planting it on the ground in intervals to give himself support as he walked without hesitation towards Randall.

"Hello, sir," shouted Randall, and embarrassingly, his tone seemed pathetic and unsure. "You're on private property. What brings you out here?"

No response came from the strange-looking man. His pace continued unbothered, and as he got closer, Randall could see that he had a weird hood over his face, making any identification of the stranger impossible. As the moon's light further illuminated his incoming visitor, the man came to a stop no more than thirty steps away.

Shifting his weight nervously on his feet, Randall spoke louder, just in case the old bastard was hard of hearing. "If you don't leave, I'm going to have to call the sheriff. I don't want to get you in any trouble, but..."

Reaching for his pocket, Randall patted the empty space where he usually carried his mobile. Scowling, he realized he had left his phone on the counter. *What a dumbass...*

Abruptly, his late-night guest pointed his walking stick directly at Randall. The gnarled piece of wood was shaped abnormally, and along its dark outline appeared to be a series of illuminated runes carved into its dark-grained surface. The effect of the backlight on the curious lettering seemed to make the symbols glow in the faint light.

From underneath the hood came the strangest raised speech, like that of some bizarre chant. The way the words sounded to Randall was like nothing he had ever heard, or in fact, had ever thought possible...it was almost like the sounds were intelligent and musical, but entirely inhuman. The melodious chant seemed like that of a voice that was speaking from another place, even from another time, and it was increasingly frightening as the otherworldly tone grew louder. The air between them seemed to grow in anticipation, as if the bizarre chorus was moving to a heightened point of release.

"Shit...fuck this," Randall shouted, and still holding his revolver, he turned and sprinted towards the house.

He was no longer a young man, but as it appeared now, Randall felt he could have given Carl Lewis a run for his money—even when he was in his prime. As he pumped his arms and concentrated on keeping his footing in the mushy ground, he ran toward the silhouetted outline of his beautiful home. For a moment, he wondered what he was going to tell his good friend Pat, who, as the only sheriff's deputy for miles around, was the authority that he would soon be on the phone with to report this crazy trespasser.

Behind him, the utterly strange chants of his unusual visitor continued, growing louder and becoming like those of an insane song from a too-loud bullhorn. The lungs that could produce such an urgent and terrifying sound could only be from an opera singer, but unlike that strong and vital tone, this came from a doddering old man in the middle of an orchard of grapes.

From some distance away, the night and remote backdrop of the winery remained calm and pleasant, but as the crescendo of the peculiar speech reached its apex, a loud crack of thunder and the flash of lightning lit up the otherwise normal night. The cacophonous boom of the event carried across the hills before fading into an odd silence.

All of which occurred under a cloudless sky.

Chapter Twenty

Several pans sizzled loudly in the cramped kitchen. Links of bubbling sausage crackled in greasy cast-iron pans, while rows of crispy bacon waited to be turned over in their own residue of bubbling oil. Near the heart-attack-inducing delicacies, numerous browned pancakes stood on an open skillet and also waited for their turn to be flipped over.

Faint salsa music drifted from the back of the kitchen in an area that housed bathrooms and the manager's office for the humble diner.

In the corner of the greasy-spoon kitchen, at a point where long-uncleaned tiles pushed up against the wall beneath a long stainless-steel sink, a small movement became evident. Moving carefully from the shadows of the dingy area, a single cockroach ventured from its hiding spot. Creeping carefully, the pest skittered into the dim light. Stopping, the insect evaluated the area. Seeming to dance on its haunches, the brave bug gyrated as it waited, perching itself on the precipice of the open kitchen area in preparation for a raid on the tasty morsels that undoubtedly lay close.

A foot smashed down on the cockroach, ending its brief life with a sickening crunch. Moving away from the scene of the crime, the cook, an overweight man wearing a sweat-stained t-shirt, briefly wiped his dirty shoe on a nearby mat in order to clean the remains of the insect from his smeared sole.

Moving to the collected remnants of food on the noisy burners, the cook scooped some hash browns and sausages onto a plate and laid them out on the collection-area divider that looked out over a simple cafe. Several plates of simple breakfasts, including scrambled eggs and omelets with buttered toasts stacked atop them, were arranged for delivery to multiple tables of customers in the eatery's scattered interior. A low murmur of varied conversations filled out the scene of what could politely be referred to as a working-class road stop.

Ringing a small bell, the cook called out in the raspy voice of a lifelong smoker. "Food's on."

Moving close with a graceful and efficient dip of her already half-full arms, a plump middle-aged woman in a clean-but-outdated uniform fetched two plates of food and moved to a corner booth of the gritty establishment. Setting down the meals, she smiled at Dani and Hideo with a polite nod before moving on to perform more of the hundred typical tasks occupying the life of a waitress in such a modest restaurant.

Nodding in turn and smiling eagerly, Hideo slid the plate directly in front of himself. As he looked down appreciatively, his eyes took on the gleam of a man that had starved for a week but soon expected his hunger to be satiated. "My favorite place…wish I could eat here every day."

Using a fork, Hideo began shuffling eggs into his mouth and grunted in flavorful ecstasy at their warm and fulfilling taste. Stopping himself, he grabbed a shaker in each hand and scattered salt and pepper on the meal, and moving on with his gourmet preparation, he squirted a generous puddle of ketchup on the pile of cooling food.

Across the booth, Dani arched a lip as she evaluated the feast. Not enamored with her meal, she pushed her own food gently to the side. "I always wondered how they make money with the $7.99 special. Seems like such…quality…should cost more."

Grunting between bites, Hideo grinned and pointed to a cup of steaming brew. "It's the high profit margins they get from the 99-cent coffee they up-sell you."

Chuckling, Dani moved the coffee in front of her and cradled it between her hands. After a last smile, her mood became focused and intense. "So…where are we at?"

Reaching to the side, Hideo pulled a folder over and opened it. Still chewing contentedly, he removed four photos and laid them on the table in front of Dani. Making sure he spaced them evenly, he pointed at the separate corpses of Darby, Bettencourt, the bodybuilder Alex, and Officer Flores, each of whom was sprawled in their own unique death pose in their varied locations.

Continuing with his meal, Hideo's appetite didn't appear to be affected by the topic and images as he spoke. "We know that the executive and the lawyer had everything to do with the deal that got Brandt Senior a new boss. That knowledge was public and easy to find."

"Yeah," Dani said, chewing on her lip, "That gives us motive. But…what about means and opportunity? You may have noticed that our portly security guard isn't seven feet tall—and he couldn't lift that axe off the ground to save his life. Also…we think Brandt ran across the musclehead near his apartment, but what about the cop? How does he fit into this?"

Holding up a fork with two speared sausages on its teeth, Hideo thought for a moment. Clearly flummoxed, he avoided gobbling down the fatty meats as he pondered their conversation. Being used to his peculiarities with eating, Dani nevertheless wanted to ram the fork into her partner's mouth, if for nothing else but to take the sight of that greasy, puke-inducing food from her view.

"No idea on him," said Hideo, and he finally scarfed down the links. "Maybe he wrote Brandt a ticket?"

Moving her gaze back to the death photos, Dani shook her head. "We're missing something. We have to get this whacko in cuffs…the captain is breathing down my neck."

"Dead cops have a way of doing that," Hideo said. "There'll be a task force soon."

Dani nodded as she twirled her coffee cup on the scratched and faded tabletop. "No doubt. But that will take time, and I would really prefer no more bodies until that point. And…we also have the matter of our own safety."

Hideo stopped chewing. "I told you that before. What's that mean now?"

Dani lowered her tone, like what came next wasn't something that should be said too loud. "It means I'm not sure we'll be safe while this plays out from…traditional investigative methods."

For the first time, Hideo lowered his fork and met her cool stare. "Yeah…go on."

"I think we need to broaden our perspective. Take him down, no matter the technicalities. It's not really that I'm a rebel, it's more that I don't want to be dead any time soon. I still have going to see Elvis' Graceland on my bucket list."

This got a grin from Hideo, but he still raised an eyebrow inquisitively. "How does that happen?"

"We start by keeping our prospective witnesses safe. Have a unit park at Miss Cooper's apartment. Babysit her everywhere she goes. Rejection is never safe when you're dealing with a nutcase."

Withdrawing his notepad, Hideo pushed his plate away and began writing as he talked. "And I'll poke around until I find out what Flores did to piss off Brandt. It can't be too hard to find."

Nodding, Dani carefully stacked the photos in front of her, then ran a fingertip over the dead face of Flores in the top picture. It was often the case that the deceased looked peaceful when they died, but in the officer's case, he looked shocked and outraged, like he wanted to complain to someone about his suddenly dead status.

After a moment, Dani looked out the window. As the night closed in on the parking lot full of beat-up cars and trucks, unhidden worry crossed her sullen face.

#

Looking into the mirror in her bathroom, Emma picked at the dark circles under her eyes. Frowning, she knew that such indications of age and fatigue were supposed to be reserved for older people, but nevertheless, here she was, feeling sorry for herself and bemoaning an already-lost youth that was neither lost nor even close to being over; indeed, she was in the prime of her younger years, yet she appeared unable to see the benefits that this time should have brought her.

Flashing a bright smile, she managed to bring back, at least for the moment, that spark of happiness that hid just under her hard surface. The smile revealed the part of her soul that she knew was there, the part that she so desperately wanted to share with a companion in life—if she could just find him.

Every day she saw people that found their other half in the world, and she was determined to make herself one of those fortunate folks that managed to live happily ever after—or at least were able to be somewhat contented in the long term.

That latest loser, Terry, had made a fleeting appearance in her life, and for the briefest of moments, she had contemplated the possibility that he was the one, and that he would be her brave knight coming to cast a light of hope into her downtrodden world.

Instead, Terry turned out to be a psycho, which in itself was not too unusual—she had known many pathetic men in her time—but there had been something else in his determined push to ingratiate himself and become part of her life that seemed even more strange than normal.

So, the police had said Terry was a stalker and had pursued other women in a similar manner in the past, though he had never been charged with anything. This was good information to know because, having become a skeptic through a lifetime of failed relationships, such knowledge had immediately crossed him off her list of mate-possibilities. However desperate she was, she was not stupid.

Anyway, there was something behind Terry's eyes that made the authority's interest in him seem not very surprising. Emma wouldn't say it was necessarily evil, but a certain badness lurked in his personality that made her realize she had just dodged a bullet by avoiding a relationship with him. It was almost as if Terry's demeanor, pathetic and weak as it always appeared, shielded something else inside his dark heart. Something she could not quite put a finger on but was nevertheless present.

Terry's strange look reminded Emma of a movie she had seen long ago, where Sean Penn had played the part of some tough kid in a juvenile detention center. There had been another young man in that prison-like environment that was constantly bullied, and that weak boy had ended up wiring a radio in order to blow up the bully's head when the hulking predator had stolen it from him. That was the feeling Emma got from Terry, that sensation that Terry would make people pay for their crimes against him, even as she also knew it was not a boombox he would use to take his revenge.

Dispirited, Emma reached down and lifted her 9mm pistol from the sink's counter. Ejecting the magazine, she proficiently checked that the chamber was loaded and slipped it into her inside-the-waistband holster under her bright-blue sweater. Grinning self-deprecatingly to herself, she noted that there was one good thing about being a larger-than-normal woman: it made it easier to carry your weapon concealed. She had long ago got the training and permit to ensure she could keep herself safe, and now was as good a time as any to make sure the weapon wasn't left uselessly at home while she was out and about.

Moving to the front door, Emma took a deep breath and opened it. Beyond the barrier was a calm and quiet night, and only a few light posts were outside to keep her company. The pathways of her tranquil complex were well-lit, but they seemed lonely for the moment, like the whole world had suddenly abandoned this area.

Shrugging, Emma moved into the night with purpose. Her simple trip to the mailboxes that occupied the middle area of the vast apartment block was not a long walk—it was one she made often—but in her mind, she felt the need to move quickly. As she paced toward the stucco-enclosed bank of mailboxes in an open square building covered under a green-tile roof, a strange sensation tickled her thoughts, as if something more than just her too-high car payment or TV bill were waiting for her there.

Halfway to the structure, Emma stopped and peered around the concrete paths that converged on her destination. Pleasant quantities of various ornamental plants and small trees lined her way ahead, but still, there was no other foot traffic or noise in the night. The lights that illuminated her way forward were bountiful and all-encompassing, yet it was almost as if something else was there as well.

On the other side of where she cautiously stood, an observer stared carefully at her through a collection of brush and branches. Crouching in the best possible area to hide himself, her watcher focused on her with rigid attention, like Emma was the only reason he was there—and the central purpose of his reason for living. Dead silent, he waited and watched.

As Emma shook her head at her paranoia and continued her walk, the dark eyes of her stalker followed her movement to the mail area. When she clicked her key into her box's lock and extracted a pile of mail, her follower skittered from under the brush and moved closer to his goal. Clothed in a frayed robe, the small figure advanced carefully, and his furtive movements left no noise as he crept forward. Professional and calm, his ability to remain quiet and unseen, even in a relatively open area such as this, was impressive.

Collecting and sorting her mail, Emma was oblivious to the hidden threat of the unseen stranger. Turning, she retraced her steps towards her apartment. She was fully aware as she walked, and her gaze moved in an arc around her, but with each of her steps toward the safety of her home, the follower was just able to pick the right spots to be shielded from her field of view.

As she got within twenty yards of her destination, Emma's pursuer moved into an alcove that was blocked from her line of sight. Blending into that recessed area, he was still and silent as he calculated his distance and certainty of success for his next actions. He would soon be able to leap upon her when she took her keys out to make entry into her apartment.

Emma was wholly unaware of his presence, and if her soon-to-be attacker timed it just right, he could seize and push her into her own residence without a peep of warning before she fell to his wicked intentions. It was just a matter of exquisite timing on the part of the soundless predator.

Abruptly, a police car screeched into view, pulling to within a scant fifty feet of her apartment door with its lights flashing. Looking up, Emma was surprised to see a brawny policeman step out of the vehicle and hurry her way. From the passenger seat, another beefy cop slid from his seat and gazed carefully around the calm and quiet area.

Stepping quickly, the driver-officer held up his hand to get Emma's attention. "Miss, may I speak with you?"

Looking relieved but not knowing why, Emma smiled in greeting and nodded to the incoming help.

Not at all far away, another set of eyes watched her make contact with the police officer and shake his hand profusely. The eyes of the stalker focused first on the cop near Emma, then over to his too-aware partner. Back and forth, the prowler's gaze moved, taking in these new threats and deciding what to do next.

Moving as quietly as before, the diminutive figure suddenly retreated into the bushes, moving noiselessly into darker areas of the complex's surroundings as he retreated. Slipping unnoticed into the peaceful night, it was as if the prowler had never been there.

Chapter Twenty-One

Terry stumbled into the kitchen and peered around with a sweaty complexion and disturbed eyes. His face was pallid and searching, like he didn't quite understand where he was or what he intended to do, and it took him a while to adjust to the uneven illumination from cheap bulbs in the ceiling's dead-bug-filled lights.

Walking haltingly to the sink, he grabbed a dirty glass from the counter and filled it with a rush from the powerful faucet. Quaffing the liquid with several extended gulps, he filled his cup with a second hit of water from the tap. After drinking more slowly until he finished, he brought himself under control by taking several deep breaths.

Terry's face had taken on the odd color of being both pale as a ghost and flushed with exertion, and he looked a bit like a corpse that had been doused in water and then reawakened from its deathly slumber. The effect on his jowly appearance was not a pleasant one, and he stood still for a moment until a more normal pigmentation returned to his skin.

Turning around, Terry's eyes focused on his father, who sat at the kitchen table with a worried look, taking in the spectacle of his son's odd demeanor and ghostly complexion. A half-eaten slice of pizza was on a plate next to Wayne, and a shot glass of clear liquid stood ready to be drunk, along with a half-full bottle of his latest vodka purchase.

Staring at his son, Wayne spoke guardedly. "You…feeling alright? You look tired."

Adjusting his gaze to Wayne, Terry had the appearance of just realizing his dad was there, like his presence was something he had just noticed in a waking dream. "Yeah…I've been getting a lot of work done."

"Work?"

"My GAME, Dad," said Terry, and his tone became contemptuous. "I'm always finding ways to improve it. It's only a matter of making every last detail perfect."

For once, Wayne hesitated to ridicule Terry's gaming activities. There was something in his son's eyes that made him stop before launching into a typical broadside of insults. Wayne was a rough person of little empathy and few good qualities, but he didn't make it to this age in life by ignoring physical cues to be wary of—especially from those that are accused of murder.

After licking his lips, Wayne hesitated a moment. Lowering his voice, he almost appeared deferential when he continued. "Listen, son…I ran into a police detective yesterday at the store. She wanted to talk about you. She said you been doin' some crazy shit."

Perking up, Terry set down his glass and stepped toward the table. His expression grew lively and inquisitive, like the conversation just grew very interesting. "And what did you tell her, Dad?"

Hesitating, Wayne licked his lips again. "Nothin'. I just wanted to know if you're into something I need to know about. Just in case we need…to get our stories straight."

Nodding, Terry took another step toward the table. His eyes focused down in an odd way, like he was making a new evaluation of Wayne. "I've been thinking about betrayal lately, Dad. The thing about betrayal is that it happens when you never quite expect it. I mean, you never get betrayed by someone you don't trust, right?"

Wayne moved his eyes down, suddenly finding it difficult to meet his son's inquiring stare. "Yeah, I guess. But family—real family—never betrays. I always taught ya that."

Taking another step, Terry stood right next to the table. "Yeah…I've been thinking about family lately, too. Thinking about MOM…and about why I never got to have her around. I thought maybe there was another reason she left. Maybe…it had nothing to do with me?"

Continuing to avoid Terry's gaze, Wayne's voice became defensive. "Bitch left me…left US. She got another man and deserted her family. You know that."

Terry pointed to the bottle of vodka. "Do I, Dad? Maybe she couldn't live with all the boozing? Maybe you beat her one time too many? Maybe…she couldn't live like that any longer…even to the point she could abandon her own son?"

Wayne finally looked up at Terry, who, although not particularly tall or imposing, seemed to hover menacingly over the table. Wayne's eyes grew pleading, and his voice wavered. "It ain't like that. I only hit her a few times—when she really had it comin'. When she was a real bitch. I was always on YOUR side, Son. I RAISED you…"

It became quiet, and Terry glowered down at his suddenly fearful father. With a lifetime of insults and abuse from the older man, the sudden reversal of their positions in their relationship was a dynamic that was unexpected and jarring for Wayne. He hadn't foreseen such a turnabout from his weak son…ever, and just now he wished he was anywhere but sitting in the same room with him.

Reaching for his shot glass, Wayne let a cautious and hopeful grin cross his face, like maybe Terry would revert to his former weakness. Like maybe they could let bygones be bygones and move back to the old way of doing things. Grabbing his drink, Wayne's hand shook with a nervous tremor as he brought the glass up to his too-dry lips.

Keeping Wayne's gaze, a menacing smile crossed Terry's face, and he slowly shook his head as his father sipped his drink.

#

Pacing carefully into the room, Dani looked down at several of her prior packed bags. The luggage from her abandoned trip to Alaska had yet to be unpacked, and her clothes and toiletries were jumbled and partially hanging out of the dusty suitcases that had spent the better part of a decade sitting unused in the garage. *I really need to travel more.*

Throughout her bedroom, Dani's decorative tastes could best have been described as subdued. On two walls were blurry photo prints of the Grand Canyon and Lake Tahoe, while on the wall above her bed was a framed written pronouncement: "Caveat Emptor—Start Drinking Early!"

Frowning, Dani started disentangling the mishmash of sweaters and T-shirts she had intended to brave the freezing wilds of Alaska with, and moving to an ancient-looking dresser, she shoved them into several crowded drawers without a thought of careful folding or proper organization.

Dani had come to like being single; there was something about being able to do what you want when you want that made life tolerable. She had forgotten the last time she actually had to worry about someone else's input on her plans and desires— be they from how to decorate her home for the holidays to whether or not she should get Indian takeout for a night of movies in front of Netflix—and such freedom of thought and action always made her crack a smile and appreciate the life of the unencumbered.

Unfortunately, she had yet to master the nuance of overcoming her feelings of loneliness, which of course was the downside to the single life. This was one reason she threw herself into her work; solving crimes meant you never had to look for dates on Tinder or whatever else people did to find companionship in today's world.

Holding that thought, Dani was reminded that she had at last promised herself to get a couple of kittens several months ago to stave off her lonely feelings. She always liked cats and how they could kind of take care of themselves, but at the same time, having to clean boxes of shit didn't strike her as particularly attractive. In fact, it seemed like doing that kind of feline maintenance was as bad as changing babies' diapers, with the added detriment that cats died too young, and even if they managed to follow you into old age, they wouldn't be able to hold your hand when you were finally gasping for your last breaths on your deathbed.

The harsh buzz of her front doorbell, pushed several times in the most annoying manner possible, interrupted her foray into self-reflection, and Dani scowled and moved toward the front door. Walking through the abandoned-looking living room, she realized it could only be Hideo that would invade her quiet space, and she began contemplating the best way to hide his body as she flung the door wide.

When she looked at her new visitor, she indeed saw that it was her erstwhile partner paying a call, but the look on Hideo's face said that he did not regret the rude interruption. His grimace and the hurried movements of his head as he gestured for her to let him inside told her this wasn't likely to be an enjoyable and comforting meeting of close friends.

Sighing, Dani motioned to the kitchen to the rear of the house and left the door open for Hideo to follow her in. As she moved into the green-painted kitchen area, full of cookie jars and pans that she had never managed to use, she slid into a chair and waited for the bad news Hideo was soon to bring.

Plopping in a chair opposite her, Hideo frowned at the cozy-looking surroundings. The stained-window oven, old stove, and fluorescent lights on the ceiling imparted a feeling of Grandma's soon-to-be-ready cooking, but Dani's shake of her head told him there would be no tasty treats forthcoming.

"Spit it out, Hideo, I have a busy schedule today. I'm thinking about shopping for cats, or at least a stuffed animal that will approximate one."

Continuing his frown, Hideo held up a manila folder and laid it carefully on the table, followed by setting a tablet computer next to it. Focusing on his partner, he stared at Dani like Armageddon had arrived, making a face that indicated a sense of abject dread had replaced his normally playful expression.

Tapping the tablet screen, Hideo moved it in front of Dani to show a scene that was both terrifying and sickening. In it, a man lay sprawled in some dirt, and his skin and flesh were scorched and shattered. One of his legs had been blown off completely, and his head was black, looking like fire engulfed the whole of his face and consumed whatever was flammable on the skull. The corpse's skin was sloughed off and black, with reddish gore streaked through the remains of charred flesh over a now-indiscernible face.

Waiting for Dani to take in the horrific photo, Hideo spoke in a serious tone. "It's Randall. I got a panicked call from Sanders about his buddy, and the Napa County Sheriff was kind enough to send over the photos after I did some inquiries."

Sitting still for some time, Dani was speechless. As she ground her jaw, a mixture of confusion and sickness came over her. Standing, she moved to the kitchen counter and flicked on the coffee maker, which responded with a light and the thrumming of heating water.

Turning around, Dani leaned back to the counter and spoke quietly. "What…happened?"

"He…got struck by lightning, on a clear night with no inclement weather, according to the forecast. One of the local deputies told me he was armed when it happened…and the barrel from his revolver was half-melted."

"It has to be the Elven mage…," replied Dani, and she drifted off for a moment before continuing in an overwhelmed whisper. "A…lightning bolt?"

Hideo scoffed, but he didn't seem convinced of his own skepticism. "It can't be. No way that could—."

"Listen to me," said Dani, her voice and eyes now suddenly alive. "We can keep pretending nothing is going on, or we can deal with this for what it is. Something we can't understand…is killing people. Something fucked up and…"

Hideo shook his head as Dani's suggestion drifted off. "If you say so…personally, I think he's got a group of psychos helping him. Just because we don't know the group or their methods doesn't mean we're in some geek version of a real-world Hell."

"A group we can't find? That now controls lightning? And nobody can see this 'group' outside of the murders?"

It became quiet as each of them fell into their own thoughts. The sound of coffee dripping from the thirty-year-old Mr. Coffee machine offered the only contrast to the silence.

Shaking his head, Hideo finally spoke up, now trying to sound upbeat. "I also spoke with the guys working the cop's murder. The officer isn't the connection—it's his wife."

"How so?"

"She worked with Brandt at a car dealership about ten years ago," said Hideo, and he now browsed through the folder, reading slowly as he looked up the specific information. "He was a security guard, and she was a…receptionist."

Dani tilted her head in confusion. "And he waited to kill her after ten years?"

"He must have a long memory. People snap all the time. Especially spurned and homicidal losers."

Doubtful, Dani thought for a moment. "Not like this, but maybe with a surrogate army doing his bidding, he's settling all his old accounts?"

Moving back to the table, Dani sat gently as she considered the circumstances of the developing case. Rubbing her hands together, she picked at her knuckles and lowered her voice. "This means I got Randall killed. I told Brandt that he was critical of him…and that put a bullseye on his back."

Hideo disagreed with a quick shake of his head. "Come on, there's no way you could've known that. Whatever is going on…you're not the one who's causing lightning strikes…or anything else."

Breathing deep, Dani crossed her arms and looked at the ceiling before continuing. "Whether you agree with me or not, we have five bodies—and Mrs. Flores is still missing. All of this is tied to Brandt, and we've got to stop him."

"We also have zero evidence of any of it. A kangaroo court wouldn't convict him."

Nodding, Dani looked down at the table. As she picked at the scratched surface, she didn't say anything, but Hideo perked up and spoke inquisitively. "How are we going to stop him, exactly?"

Meeting his gaze, Dani looked determined. With not a hint of doubt in her voice, she motioned toward the front door and the wider world. "I'll meet you at his complex at seven PM. Whatever it takes, this psycho is done. I'm not waiting to be his next victim, and neither should you."

Chapter Twenty-Two

Foot traffic was light in the apartment complex's shadowy parking lot. Faint light came from a series of old lampposts, but in many of the copper-looking light structures were several receptacles that lacked light bulbs entirely. By the dilapidated look of the wider property, however, the old and handcrafted metal lights were actually the most attractive features of the derelict environment.

Detective Harrod squinted through his windshield as he tried to focus on Terry's distant building. Sitting in the interior of an old department sedan that had seemingly been used since before the 49ers won their first Super Bowl, he didn't stick out as a cop in the lower-class environment; in fact, he looked a bit like a homeless guy settling into his car for a night of recreational people-watching.

With etched frown lines that gave away his deep middle age and an attitude that bred an atmosphere of boredom, Harrod wasn't going to win a prize for the most diligent public servant any time soon. Reclining in the cracked leather of the front seat, he breathed a sigh of sorrowful reservation at his choice of career. *Only three more years until retirement.*

Reaching carefully over, he grabbed a crinkled bag of Doritos and began shoveling them into his mouth. Crunching on the chunks of nutrition-less chips, he scowled at the stale taste from a bag left unattended for too long.

"How you doing, Harrod?" asked Dani, and the surprised detective spun his head to look out the window into the face of the much-younger homicide inspector. She returned his gaze with a playful smile, one that showed they both were a bit surprised at her turning up at the stakeout.

Behind Dani, Hideo stood rather sheepishly between two cars, and he held a pair of binoculars at his side as he flashed a not-too-assertive smile.

"What're you two doing here?" asked Harrod, and confused, he quietly opened the door and leaned out of the car to get a better view of his colleagues. "I thought Collins was gonna relieve me?"

Dani leaned close, keeping her grin and affecting an *I'm your best buddy impression* as she pointed to Hideo. "Collins is on the other side of the apartments, so I doubt he's going to break you. We're gonna break you both instead, so take an hour and get some real food. I heard that Italian place over on Broadway is running a special for cops."

Harrod started to extricate himself from his seat, seemingly thinking something was amiss with the strange changeover in his surveillance duties, but after a moment of uncomfortable struggles, he shrugged and gave up. Easing himself into his seat again, he pulled the door shut and motioned toward Terry's place. "Shit, sounds good, I guess…don't gotta tell me twice. Have fun."

Stepping aside, Dani and Hideo watched Harrod back out of the unlit space under the dead-bulbed light post and turn toward the parking lot's exit. As his clunky car accelerated and merged into traffic, Harrod's headlights flicked on.

Looking expectantly over at Dani, Hideo raised his eyebrows. "Now what?"

#

Minutes later, Hideo and Dani crouched behind a row of untrimmed hedges. Light from a strong moon and plentiful stars made the area around them somewhat visible, but the dim area's location alongside a collection of dumpsters was largely nondescript and provided good cover.

Breathing in, Dani realized they must look pretty ridiculous here, if indeed anyone was even taking the time to notice two cops sneaking around dumpsters in this shitty part of town. If they had been creeping around like this in a well-to-do area of the city, she imagined a 911 call would have been par for the course, but here it was more likely that the neighborhood cats would be the only residents to notice their covert behavior.

Wriggling his nose at the unpleasant odor of uncollected refuse, Hideo pointed across the unkempt landscaping of untrimmed lawns and overgrown brush towards Terry's modest apartment block. He whispered carefully, revealing his discomfort with their current situation and shady legal standing. "Are you ready? Don't screw this up—I like this job...and my freedom."

Staring at the building, Dani took in the lack of movement from the sliding glass door to the front of the single-story apartment home. Lights peaked from behind cheap curtains through the glass, but no other movement or indication of who occupied the place was evident. Clearly, there was no party going on in the Brandt household, but that wasn't exactly a surprise when she considered the social skills of their target.

Looking uncomfortable and speaking quietly, Dani nodded. "I always wondered how criminals felt when they were ready to do their criminal thing. Now, I get to experience the same feeling...kinda wish I had just played *Grand Theft Auto* instead."

Chuckling, Hideo nodded and held up his wrist to check the time on his watch. "OK, we got about fifty minutes. Just make sure you—."

Stopping, Hideo held up a finger and motioned to his radio earpiece. His face went cold as his voice sank into a worried tone. "Shit, the unit at Emma Cooper's place isn't responding."

Chapter Twenty-Three

Emma's vastly more attractive apartment complex was also devoid of foot traffic in the late evening. But here, the lights from an array of black metal posts shone without malfunction, and the concrete footpaths around the vicinity's squat two-story buildings were clean and bordered by groomed flower beds and healthy-looking plants.

At the front of the property, a police car was backed into a space that kept it within easy view of Emma's apartment. To either side of the vehicle were orange cones blocking off three spaces, ensuring the immediate area was clear of too many onlookers and giving the cop car space to allow for a secure overwatch of the pleasant neighborhood.

The car appeared to be unoccupied, but closer in, it was obvious there was good cause for Hideo's concern about the sudden interruption of communication with Emma's protective detail. The windows of both sides of the cruiser were open, and across the interior of the windshield, a spray of dark blood dripped and ran down the glass.

In the driver's seat, the reclined and dark form of a policeman was just visible in the dim light, and one of his arms jutted at such an angle that it hung out over the edge of the window's open frame. Rivulets of his blood streamed and dripped to the asphalted ground from his extended fingers, and the cop's hand convulsed intermittently in a sign his nerves were releasing their grip on life.

From the passenger's seat, from a position that had less illumination, another cop's form kicked and struggled amidst more splashed blood and gore. There was some life left in this police officer, and gurgles and gasping from some unseen and grievous wounds to the man's throat were the primary evidence of his continued survival. But from the descending sounds of his hacks and grunts for breath, this was also a person whose injuries were mortal and would soon be joining his partner in death.

Throughout the rest of the surroundings, the area was quiet, as if there was no apparent cause for concern in the unoccupied exterior area of the otherwise normal night.

#

Terry sat at rigid attention in his kitchen, his arms perched firmly on the surface of the wooden table. Focusing down, his eyes were again elsewhere, and a disturbing and detached grin was pasted across his sweating and ashen face. His eyes, the eyes of an engrossed and fanatical believer, mirrored the soul of one who had lost all connection with empathy or human feeling.

The small painted and lifelike figure of the ghoul stood below him, and, stuck in the ravenous pose of an undead predator, looked unique and terrifying in the scant illumination of the partially-lit kitchen. Its razor-sharp claws, tipped with just the right amount of red paint to produce a bloody sheen, appeared utterly real and distinctly dangerous.

More bloody fragments of painted, discolored flesh were speckled on the tattered clothes that the ghoul wore, showing something like the clothes of a peasant that had been worn into shreds from time spent in wretched and dirty conditions. The elongated mouth of its zombie-like face bristled with long teeth that were also tipped in blood, and its eyes were opened wide and intelligent, with just a glint of silver hue to evoke self-awareness and calculated malevolence.

The figure sat on top of one of his open-paged monster manuals, where a drawing on the page below it looked precisely like the miniature. Terry seemed to glare through the figure, as if the spirit of the inanimate object was unified with his fugue state.

Perspiration continued to dribble down Terry's face as his mind obsessed uniformly on some unknown and wicked goal, and his attention and focus were on somewhere or something far removed from this dim kitchen.

\#

Sitting on her couch, Emma was engrossed in a house-hunting program on the wall-mounted TV. The show was the type where the buyers were as fake as their prospective properties, at least in the sense that she doubted these people actually shopped for these specific apartments themselves. She loved these types of reality programs, but on this particular international edition, she couldn't quite figure out why there were only three houses to choose from—in Prague, of all places. *Weren't there like a million people living there?*

Truth was, it always seemed to Emma that people put far too much stock in buying a place. First, you needed a bunch of money that had to be used for a down payment—and that was usually tens of thousands of dollars she had never had in her whole life—then you had to shop for your place, bargain with some owner that always wanted more, then sign away your life in order to call a house "your own." After that, you paid insurance and maybe bought payment protection, which would have set her back even more from her piss-poor paycheck. By the time she would be done, she would be chained to the place and never able to move anywhere else. Even when the point came and she was an old lady with no mortgage, she still would owe HOA fees and property taxes, so how could people ever say that something was truly "paid off?" The whole thing kind of seemed like a scam.

She could, of course, find a roommate to split the costs, but that meant having no privacy and kind of ruined the reason for purchasing a home in the first place. Or, she could find a man to help with the costs, as well as provide other benefits, but that hadn't quite worked out the way she had hoped.

Sighing, Emma reached over and pulled a bear-claw pastry from the plastic wrapper of a package she had bought at the local bakery. Taking a bite of the scrumptious filling and almond-coated snack, she nodded at its delicious taste, while also realizing her diet would have to wait for another day.

From outside came the abrupt scream of a voice—that of a terrified woman. The long and horrified wail of the unseen lady was like nothing Emma had ever heard, like the person was losing her mind in real time. It seemed like an amplified version of a soon-to-be-killed starlet in some scary movie, only earthier and more authentic. In the calm of this quiet neighborhood, the shrieks were shocking and out of place.

Standing upright from her couch, Emma looked warily toward her front door, then at the small window that faced the main parking area of the complex. She couldn't decide if that opening was big enough to admit a home-invader, but she didn't really want to find out. The cries of that lady dissipated somewhat, like she was running away from the area, but Emma could still hear her overwhelmed whimpers as the anonymous female retreated from the nearby area.

Her mind racing, Emma quickly moved from the living area to her bedroom, where she bent down to a firearm safe that served as an end table next to her bed. Long ago, when she had a loser-stalker that couldn't take "no" for an answer, she had invested in the safe and her gun as a guarantor of her future safety. Now she just kept a small tablecloth over the heavy-framed box, and it actually looked decent as a holding space for her chips or romance novels while she relaxed in bed.

Quickly punching in her birthday as the code, the safe door whirled and clicked open, and Emma snatched her thin semiautomatic weapon from the padded inside. In a mild panic, anxiety crept through her whole body for a moment, and she tried to contain the fear in her arms as she fought off the shakes in her suddenly weary limbs.

Walking carefully back to the front of the apartment, she kept the pistol pointed down but at the ready as she peered expectantly ahead. After a while of staring dumbly at the door, Emma started to feel stupid for the whole effort. Whatever had happened outside, there was no longer any screaming, and she didn't know how long she planned to gawk at the door, looking like an idiot in her own empty apartment.

Relaxing her grip, she let the gun point directly down and took a deep breath. *Whatever happened, it ain't about me, at least.*

The sudden and very strong THUD of an impact on her door brought her back to reality. The force of the blow was jarring, and it left her with no doubt that whatever was outside was now coming for a visit to her personally. Several more blows against the door followed, and Emma thanked God she had seen fit to have a steel-framed door installed at that long-ago point in her stalker-filled past.

Except, even with the added strength of the reinforced door, the frame was still giving way under the strident force of the fierce blows. Eyes wide, Emma raised her pistol and pointed it toward the weakening barrier. Shouting, she tried to keep control of her rising fear. "Who are you…what do you want? I got a gun, and I'll blow you the fuck away."

The top of the heavy door splintered inward, having been cracked entirely open. Off-kilter, the door was now partially off its frame, and shards of wood were peeled off and jutting out from its metal core. For a moment, it was quiet, like whoever was directly outside had heard and heeded Emma's warning.

Suddenly, a bizarre and off-gray hand, topped with vicious claws and covered in blood, reached through the narrow opening. Grasping down, the elongated fingers scratched across the thick door as it tried to grab the knob below. The length of the arm was odd, appearing too long for its frame, like it was twice the scale of a normal person's limb. The vile flesh of the soon-to-be intruder's arm was marked with striated veins, and its strange paleness showed the hideous appendage to be anything but human.

With a CRACK CRACK CRACK, Emma pulled the trigger and fired as quickly as her finger would allow, sending a host of booming shots at the fetid thing trying to break into her home.

#

At his table, Terry's distant look began to show emotion. A leering and wretched grin crossed his face, causing his mottled skin to appear like a perverse corpse. He was no longer a reserved and pathetic loser, but instead a savage and unstoppable predator. He knew it, and more importantly, someday…all his enemies would as well.

The thrill of the hunt and a sense of justice for avenging his past inadequacies flowed through Terry's mind, and for a moment, he was in two places, both with his alter-self in the ghoul's body and here in his dumpy, dark kitchen.

They had all conspired against Terry, spending their lives making fun of him, beating him up, and laughing at the mere notion that he could find a way to live amongst the cool and intelligent people in society. Whether as a boy or a man, the only time people were kind or showed feigned respect for him was when they pitied him or wanted something. The waitresses that served him food only grudgingly smiled in appealing for a tip, while even the whores he picked up to satisfy his urges weren't enthusiastic in their duties, as if money alone couldn't make him a real man in their sex-worker world.

As self-satisfaction helped take away the pain of a lifetime of rejection, Terry considered his single-minded form of entertainment, which had now morphed into how he would take his vengeance. As a young boy he had picked up the hobby of role-playing gaming, and from that time, it had come to dominate his life, serving as the vehicle to dampen his shame and push back at the world from its incessant tendency to harm and denigrate him.

Wherever he tried to play by their rules, Terry was lambasted and belittled, given only the jobs others didn't want, and only openly tolerated with a roll of the eyes or a dismissive grin. A life spent being ignored and found wanting by prospective friends and women alike plagued Terry and forced him to accept his diminished place in the world.

But now that was changing. Never again would they laugh, or else they would pay the price from his new and unique abilities. His hate for those out there, all those superior, moneyed pricks and dismissive bitches, would now percolate and fuel his unending wrath. His justice and ability to wreak unceasing havoc on the powerful in this new world would make them all tremble. They would know fear and despair for how they looked down and mocked others. He would return their pain ten-fold for their crimes against him and others.

The best part, of course, was nobody could blame or stop Terry as he righted all those wrongs. The sky was truly the limit when you killed without evidence, and he relished all the ways he would plan and purge those who so richly deserved their just endings. Better yet, he would impose his revenge with the "fake" monsters he had used in his gaming world for all these lonely years.

Grinning, Terry knew the whole thing was almost too perfect, and he leaned eagerly forward to gaze at his miniature ghoul. Getting so close as to almost kiss the figure, his leer continued, and focusing elsewhere, he prepared to finish off his recent love interest, Emma, with a final and gleeful rush into her home.

From behind him, a flash of metal and a vicious thud as something careened into his skull. Sprawling forward, Terry collapsed onto the linoleum floor. Turning over and trying to look up, he uttered a mewling, guttural sound as he tried to understand what had just happened. Grasping a half-clenched hand upward, he saw a blurry and indistinguishable face hovering in the faint light. *What...who?*

Unable to reach the stranger, his strength wilted away, and his shaky view of the world descended into darkness. Going limp, his murderous rampage was momentarily interrupted.

Stepping closer, Dani held a heavy revolver in her firm grip. Still grasping her weapon by its stainless-steel 4-inch barrel, she peered down at the crumpled Terry with a mix of contempt and satisfaction.

#

Dani cast a large cup of water into Terry's face, then moved quickly behind him. Sitting at a chair next to the kitchen table, Terry's arms were thoroughly tied behind it with various computer cords, barely allowing for movement.

Terry slowly came awake and shook his head. His skin's pallor was now normal, with that extraordinary, otherworldly tone now replaced by his ruddy and unwashed complexion. His scruff of poor beard growth, creating a half-present manliness which didn't impress for its masculinity, topped off his return to his normal self.

With his head lulling, Terry tried to focus on the area around him. Dani was not visible, so he arched his neck to see who was in the room behind him. He caught the shadow of the detective standing there but couldn't quite make out her face.

"All of this…because you didn't like the way you were treated?" asked Dani, still not coming into his view.

Terry focused on the table in front of him, where a deep cooking pan was piled high with his numerous miniature monsters and characters. Jumbled together, they didn't seem so real or scary now; instead, they appeared like childish toy things.

Coming fully awake, Terry groaned at the pain in his head, and recognizing Dani's voice, he stuttered out a response. "How…are you here? What's happening?"

Stepping into view, Dani set an empty bottle of vodka on the table. The tough glass of the sturdy container was smeared with darkish blood.

Notably, Dani was wearing plastic gloves, the type used when handling evidence from a crime scene. Regarding Terry with derision, the same sort he had been shown his entire life, she spoke coldly. "I'm here to stop you, you miserable loser. I think the world has had about enough of you. I know Elk Grove and Sacramento certainly have."

Terry avoided her glare, and his eyes darted to the bottle.

Dani nodded, and exasperated, she raised her voice. "You even killed your own father? He was an asshole, but who does that?"

Glancing over to the living room, Dani motioned to Wayne, who was sprawled awkwardly over the couch with only one leg jutting up at a strange angle. His cherished kitten was trying to pet itself against his leg as it purred, oblivious to Wayne's deceased status.

Terry's eyes teared up as he spoke defensively. "He was going to betray me…just like everyone——."

"He was protecting you, you childish moron. He wouldn't tell me anything. Your one ally in your shitty, pathetic life, and you killed him."

Licking his lips, Terry steeled his jaw at her statement, as if ignoring Dani's logic would make it less true. Staying quiet, it didn't appear he wanted to discuss his dad at the moment.

Shaking her head, Dani set a large buck knife, a rather cheap but perilously sharp one, next to the bottle in front of him. Terry eyed the knife warily.

"I thought I was going to have to find an excuse to shoot you," said Dani, and she sighed in a clinical way, like it was all part of a day's work. "After you tried to 'stab' me. I'm not into felonies or framing people, so I wasn't sure how to pull it off. It's really the kind of thing you only see in movies."

Fearful, Terry continued staring at the knife.

"But you saved my ass, Terry," she continued. "We now got you dead to rights for killing your dad, so I won't have to go all 'black ops' on you."

Slowly moving his head, Terry chanced a gaze at Dani. Her face was almost amused, but her eyes were cold.

"I want a doctor…and a lawyer. You can't do any of this. I have rights."

Dani smiled at the irony of that. Just as with all criminals, no matter how smart or calculating, they always fell back on society's rules when their chickens came home to roost. It was a sad statement on society that it usually worked, too.

But she wasn't having any of it. With a vicious smack, she slapped Terry's chubby face. Shocked by the action, Terry blinked his eyes, and more tears formed as blood bubbled and ran from his nose.

"First things first," said Dani, feeling proud of herself for the assault. It wasn't every day you got to smack a murderer. "Tell me how you did it. You have some kind of evil power from these figurines? Some kind of witchcraft? I've never been too much of a believer in the occult, but somehow, you've managed to change my mind. Funny how unsolvable murders can do that."

Staring at his pile of figures, there was a certain rebelliousness forming in Terry's expression, like that of one who, whatever his weaknesses, had decided to make a stand on something. Shaking his head, he stayed quiet. The trickle of blood down his lip actually made him look brave for a moment.

After a long sigh, Dani continued, but she lowered her voice, as if sharing a secret with the helpless man. "The question I have to ask myself, Terry, is, should I just kill you? I can't have whatever you've been doing happen to me or my partner—or anyone else, for that matter. I'm a boring person, so that's a bit too exciting a prospect for me."

Looking back up at Dani, Terry focused on her with unhidden hatred. Now it was not a fearful man that engaged her eyes, but the stare of an unrepentant killer. True, it wasn't a sadistic murderer in the normal sense, but his motivations and lack of mercy were just the same.

Rolling her eyes and breathing deep, Dani walked from his view for a moment. Returning quickly, she set a soldering torch on the table. The stack of things accumulating there made Terry's gaze move from one to the next with some confusion.

"Or, should I just torture you until you tell me everything?" Dani asked. "You like to cause pain to others, but what happens when the tables are turned?"

Reaching down, Dani triggered the igniter on the bottle. Holding it up, she moved it close to Terry's face, where his eyes went wide as he stared at the flame. The light from its whooshing fire illuminated his rotund features, showing panic and fear in his eyes.

But there was also defiance, and Dani was impressed for the first time since coming to know the ample-framed man. Faced with his end, he actually grew a set of balls and stuck up for himself. True, it was in defense of wanton killing, but she really hadn't thought he had it in him.

Grinning coldly, Dani twisted the knob and increased the stream of fire as she held Terry's gaze. Holding the lengthy flame even closer to his face, she let her smile toy with his fears.

Shrugging, Dani turned to the table, where she directed the searing flame of the torch onto his pile of figures. Moving the flame over each, she began to melt them down, immolating them one by one. As she did so, Terry began to panic, and he pulled against his constraints as each of his precious miniatures was reduced to puddles of molten lead and metal.

It didn't take long, but by the time Dani was done, Terry finally showed something like trauma and intense grief on his stricken face, as if someone had finally inflicted emotional pain on a person who had steeled himself from such feelings over a lifetime of misery and self-loathing.

Going limp, Terry stared blankly at what remained, letting his face go slack as he took in the loss. Moving behind him, Dani untied his bindings, and drawing her revolver, threw him face down on the couch. As she handcuffed him and cinched the metal cuffs tight, Terry's face was not that far from his father's body, and a single tear ran from his eye as she finished the arrest. It wasn't readily apparent if the tear was for his destroyed game-toys or his dead father, but his face hardened as he submitted himself to this unceremonious end of his criminal career.

Keying the radio she carried, Dani spoke in a professional tone to Hideo. "Call it in. I've taken him into custody."

Chapter Twenty-Four

Eleven months later, the sun shone brightly on the same town of Elk Grove. At a busy intersection on a wide, four-lane street, assorted cars zoomed along the road as people went about their personal business on a mellow and relaxing Saturday afternoon.

Off that main thoroughfare was an attractive and well-attended strip mall. Rows of expensive sedans and SUVs were parked in its wide parking lot, and a cross-section of browsing people attended to their shopping needs and other errands in food establishments, coffee shops, and specialty stores.

In the corner of the pleasant outdoor mall, a particular eatery and bar was especially busy at this normally sedate time of day. A simple sign above the place read "Sports Pub and Grill." Several police cars were parked near the business' front entry doors, while farther from the main entrance was parked Hideo and Dani's unmarked police car.

Inside, unobtrusive country music played in the background, and the layout of the establishment included multiple tables and numerous TVs playing various sports matches on bright and subtitled screens.

At a long table underneath a bank of screens sat Dani and Hideo. Trays of nachos and half-eaten chicken wings were splayed out before them, and several nearby police officers stood around eating from the entrées and sipping from glasses of soda and other non-alcoholic drinks.

The mood was somewhat hopeful, like it was a graduation day for college students, but a certain seriousness stood just behind the light environment. The combination of people was usually not in celebration mode at such a place and time, and the conversation and backdrop were subdued, with each of the cops present mulling over bittersweet thoughts as they considered the sorrowful moment.

Pointing to the screen, Hideo cleared his throat and held up a remote to raise the volume on what was soon to be announced from one of the TVs. As the surrounding conversations died down, the host of other law enforcement officers raised their eyes to focus on an image of a courthouse.

From the State Justice Building, a crowd of people emerged. Lawyers and courthouse guards escorted a handcuffed Terry Brandt from the entrance, and crowds of journalists and interested onlookers jockeyed to ask questions of him and his attorneys. With no answers forthcoming from the harried defense team, the sounds of the mob died down and were replaced by the sharp and clear voice of an unseen news anchor:

"…it has yet to be seen how that will play out. Yesterday, Terry Brandt was convicted of first-degree murder, and he now faces a sentence of life without parole for the killing of his father, Wayne Brandt.

Known as the 'RPG Killer,' Mr. Brandt is suspected in at least seven other homicides in the Capitol Region, including those of several police officers, but the District Attorney has yet to bring charges in those cases, citing a lack of material evidence.

Authorities continue to ask that anyone with information on the other deaths come forward immediately, as it is suspected that multiple other suspects could be involved in this sensational case…"

Killing the sound, Hideo lowered the remote. Looking somber, he held up his Ginger Ale and spoke up in a respectful tone. "To our brothers who fell. You will always be with us. Rest with God."

Mournful smiles came from all around as the other cops agreed with sad nods and heavy hearts. As the low-key conversations around them restarted, the place took on the vibe of a celebration of life. Even if the dead were unknown to everyone who was present, they each shared the communal bond of those who willingly risked their lives for the public good.

Smiling fondly at her partner, Dani heard the DING of an incoming text from the phone in her pocket. Pulling out her mobile, she began reading the unseen communication. After a moment, she moved to the corner of the room for some privacy and continued reading. The color from her face drained as she worked through the message, and her expression changed from detached enjoyment of the moment to hesitant trepidation.

Hideo noticed the silent exchange, and he rose and moved over to find the cause. Leaning close to Dani, he kept his voice low. "What is it?"

Frowning, Dani nodded to the television. "It's Brandt, through his lawyer. He wants to meet with us; he said he needs to 'get something off his chest.'"

Hideo scowled, processing the information with a doubtful tilt of his head. "Really? You think he found a conscience? He just got convicted yesterday…maybe he wants to rat someone out?"

Thinking for a moment, Dani grimaced and shook her head. Not knowing what Terry wanted was worrisome, but she knew it would have to be checked out, if only to help close out the case. She suspected the world would never know or believe what really happened with this case, but she might as well see what Brandt wanted.

Suddenly of a negative mindset, Dani looked back to the trays of food and drinks. The brief mood of communal reverence now seemed to be gone.

#

Later that night, lights from multiple perimeter watchtowers illuminated the surroundings of the main holding jail in Sacramento, California. To the interior of the powerful beams, an enormous concrete building was linked to several other out-structures, making the voluminously lit central area appear like a concrete bunker attached to snake-like wooden outbuildings.

Surrounding the structures were two concentric rings of barbed razor wire-topped fences, which appeared rather odious under the clouds of bugs that circled the huge lamps above them.

Inside the jail was a sterile and loud environment. White halls, clean and shining under more lights, squeaked under the shoes of Dani and Hideo as they trudged toward the facility's main interview room. Looking worried and not knowing what to expect, they traded concerned glances as they trailed behind an imposing guard.

Stopping, the immense and portly guard inserted a key into the lock of a nondescript door and moved out of the way. Uninterested in their specific intentions for the prisoner in the room, he didn't make eye contact as he waived the detectives inside.

Stepping through the doorway, Dani and Hideo were greeted by another bright room, and sitting behind a large metal table was the hapless Terry Brandt. The wall along one side of the empty room was occupied by a huge one-way mirror, and there were two chairs facing the criminal they had so struggled to capture. Stepping closer, Dani appraised the murdering psychopath with a stern grimace.

Terry motioned with a grin for them to sit, his beaming smile indicating his happiness at seeing them again. Not since the long trial had they laid eyes upon him in person, and as indicated by his good complexion and easy-going demeanor, confinement seemed to be treating him well. Aside from his cuffed hands connected to a short chain that anchored him to the sturdy table, he looked like an old buddy greeting beloved friends.

Unaccompanied by an attorney, which Terry had set as a precondition to this same-day meeting, he waved kindly for them to sit. "Thanks for coming. You must've been busy lately."

Sliding into the cold chair across from him, Dani was dismissive. "Terry, cut the BS. Just tell us what you want."

Sitting down in his own chair, Hideo scooted close to the table. He held his hand up, as if to mediate a contentious meeting, and pulled his ubiquitous notepad from a suit jacket. "Now now…relax, Dani. I'll start first, OK?"

Offering Terry a fake smile, Hideo fell into his amused expression, the one that informed most of what he did in life. "Now Terry, I have news for you that you'll be happy to hear. I just talked to Emma, your old girlfriend."

Terry's face brightened, and he replied with a curious rise of his eyebrows.

Hideo flipped through a few papers, then nodded with an *Aha* as he found his notes. "She told me to tell you are a 'pathetic asshole, and she hopes that you rot in hell.' She had other colorful words, but I think you get the gist of our conversation. I'm afraid to say, I don't think there'll be a rapprochement between you two any time soon. It's not likely she'll be waiting for you to get out…ever. Not that you will get out, of course."

Terry's merry temperament melted away with the information. Pursing his lips, Terry leaned as close as his cuffed hands would allow. "You guys don't have to be jerks to me. In your own way, you were honorable enemies. You were just doing your jobs."

Dani gave an ironic chuckle and raised her voice. "Gee, that's nice, Terry, it's almost like we used to play chess, instead of you butchering people. Let's get on with this."

Returning her smile, Terry peered innocently at Dani. "With what?"

"Your confession," said Dani, growing impatient. "Come clean—be a man, instead of the freak you are. Tell us how you did—."

"Why on earth would I confess, Detective? No…now we can start a new game."

Continuing his wry grin, Terry moved his gaze between the partners, like they all were having a relaxing cup of tea, and he couldn't wait to tell them some new and exciting news.

"Game?" asked Hideo, for the first time showing some impatience. "What are you talking about?"

"The same as before," replied Terry, sounding sure of himself—despite his current predicament of being convicted and incarcerated. "You can try to figure out who or what is killing people. All the ones out there that most deserve it."

Scoffing, Dani leaned forward. "However you did it before, that isn't going to happen, you prick. I burned all your figures to slag."

Staring over at Dani, Hideo looked at her like she was as crazy as Brandt.

Holding his hand out, Terry dropped six paper-created figures from his palm on the table. They were crudely made, but they approximated assorted monsters and people, just like with his old miniatures.

As the partners stared down at the small origami-like creations, Terry spoke with some enthusiasm. "These are nice, aren't they? They don't let me have metal in here, so I have to be creative. It doesn't really matter, though, 'cuz I can make new ones every night."

Confused, Dani stared searchingly at Terry. She plucked up one of the figures, and turning it over between her fingers, she could see it was oddly shaped. Staring at its dimensions and the short nature of its cutout hair, it almost appeared to look like herself, of all things.

Terry clicked his tongue and sounded cheerful, just as he recognized the understanding that came over Dani's face. "It was never about the figures, Detective. It was always about my book, the one that I just got back yesterday from the state, thanks to my attorneys. You see, California has to let you read, no matter how long the sentence."

Terry's smile deepened, even as a far more malignant intention filled his glowering eyes. For once, he seemed pleased and happy to be alive. Life was now at its most meaningful point for him, like he had finally found his calling, his reason for living. He spoke softly, letting the newfound joy of the moment fill his face with anticipation. "And now I have the rest of my life to play with it."

The End

About the Author

Tim lives in Nevada, where he makes a life enjoying all things horror and thriller-related, from films to books, and even the occasional convention. He has three children, three cats, and he enjoys providing reading entertainment for the monster and creature-loving masses.

If you like this novel, he would appreciate a review or a follow on Facebook:
https://www.facebook.com/Horrorthrillerguy
https://www.horrorthrillerguy.com
Also by Timothy Bryan:
Chindi
books2read.com/u/mlAJ7Z
The Huntsman of Corvinus
books2read.com/u/mVRyr5
Despicable
books2read.com/u/49k0ak
By Their Cold Fingers
books2read.com/u/bPgMKr
Prisoners of a Dark Night
books2read.com/u/mllzqW

www.ingramcontent.com/pod-product-compliance
Lightning Source LLC
Chambersburg PA
CBHW061230310726
48971CB00007B/2009